CHAMPION OF THIEVES . . .

Phillipe sat back on his knees, gaping at this unexpected rescuer, with his fierce, golden-eyed hawk and his magnificent black war-horse. He held a gleaming broadsword in his free hand, and the cold blue eyes that shone in his shadowed face were as distant and threatening as the land of Death. Phillipe tore his gaze away from the silent figure and looked back over his shoulder at the guardsmen who'd been pursuing him.

The two men sat on their horses, momentarily frozen with awe. At last one roused himself and said, "Clear the bridge. The man's an escaped prisoner. We're taking him in."

"On whose authority?" the stranger asked at last.

"His Grace, the Bishop of Aquila."

Only Phillipe saw the fleeting, involuntary twitch of the stranger's mouth that might have been a smile. Then the war-horse lunged forward, the hawk rose shrieking into the air. . . .

SIGNET Science Fiction You'll Enjoy

LADYHAWKE

Joan D. Vinge

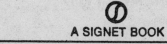

A SIGNET BOOK

NEW AMERICAN LIBRARY

SIGNET TRADEMARK REG. U.S. PAT. OFF. AND FOREIGN COUNTRIES
REGISTERED TRADEMARK—MARCA REGISTRADA
HECHO EN CHICAGO, U.S.A.

SIGNET, SIGNET CLASSIC, MENTOR, PLUME, MERIDIAN and NAL BOOKS
are published by New American Library,
1633 Broadway, New York, New York 10019

First Printing, March, 1985

1 2 3 4 5 6 7 8 9

PRINTED IN THE UNITED STATES OF AMERICA

For "Billy and Duff"

Chapter One

At sunrise the rider in black was waiting on the hilltop far above the city, as he had waited there the dawn before, and the dawn before that. He shifted in his saddle, cold and weary, watching the sky brighten and the gray morning fog lift from the valley below.

As the mists parted, he saw the crenellated towers of Aquila Castle break into view, fleetingly golden, like a glimpse of heaven. For a moment the sight made him ache with longing. Only for a moment. He smiled mirthlessly at his own inability to stop believing this vigil would someday have an end, or show him an answer.

Below him now the rest of the ancient city emerged from the fog. Aquila had been a thriving town since Roman times—it still bore the old Roman name, which meant "Eagle." But the Middle Ages had confined its cramped houses and twisting, narrow streets inside grim walls of stone, surrounded them with a moat of black, sluggish water fed by an underground river.

The fields outside the city gates were nearly as bleak. Autumn had come early this year, after a blistering summer with almost no rain. The year before had been no better. By now the fields had been harvested of whatever poor, drought-stunted crops had survived. This year's harvest would scarcely have fed the already-hungry people of Aquila through the winter, even if their Bishop had not raised taxes again, to keep his own storehouses and coffers full. The specter of famine haunted the dreary streets of the city. But while the Church Militant ruled, the people paid, and starved.

Only the cathedral, lying at the city's heart, still kept its ethereal beauty in the full light of day. High windows of colored glass and countless silken pennants turned its saint-lined walls and vaulted ceilings into a vision of paradise—the closest most of the worshipers gathered there for Mass would ever get to heaven on earth. The Bishop promised them their reward in the next world, while he enjoyed his now.

The gaunt, candlelit faces of the citizens of Aquila gazed impassively toward the altar, resigned to their prayers. Organ music filled the vast space above them and overflowed into the streets, reaching even the watcher on the hill.

The Bishop of Aquila stood before the ornate altar, a severely resplendent figure in his white brocaded robes. He chanted the Credo of the Mass in a high-pitched, toneless singsong that was more a warning than a promise of redemption. The worshipers mouthed the obligatory Latin responses, meaningless words they had memorized by rote. If any of them had dared to look directly at him, they would have gazed uneasily on the contrast between the richness of his clothing and the unhealthy pallor of his angular features. He was a tall man, well into middle age, with a face that showed the signs of years of self-indulgent living, and glittering eyes as pale and unforgiving as ice.

He turned toward the two altar boys who stood waiting beside him; they held out a jewel-encrusted golden chalice for his blessing. He had told his congregation that this was the Holy Grail, and in his mind it was beautiful enough that it should have been. He had paid enough for it that it should have been. He was a man with a highly refined appreciation of beauty.

He held out his beringed hand to the two boys, glancing down at the ring as he did. It was solid gold, so large and heavy that it fit only on his thumb. Its plain, massive setting held a perfect emerald the size of an olive. The ring alone had cost him a small fortune, drawn, of course, from the wealth he had squeezed from the faithful in the name of God. But God's needs were neither as worldly nor as expensive as his own.

As the boys kissed the ring and backed away, a dull crack, like the echo of a shot, rang through the cathedral. The Bishop glanced toward an unshuttered window. The dangling legs of three bodies swung silently from a gallows, just outside Aquila Castle across the city square. Organ music swelled around him again, and he turned back unconcernedly to the Mass.

Meanwhile, out in the square, a small crowd of Aquila's less devout citizens had gathered. They goggled up at the limp, hanging bodies of three thieves who had abruptly made their own peace with God. The four guardsmen who were in charge of bringing out more prisoners for execution stood warily among them, waiting for further orders from their captain. Their crimson-and-black uniforms stood out in bloody contrast to the drab, patched clothing of the crowd.

Marquet, the Captain of the Guard, was a brutal man with a dark beard and eyes as hard as his disposition. His blunt, heavily muscled body looked as if it had been born to commit mayhem and violence. Marquet had been their leader for two years, since their former captain had been charged with treason by the Bishop and outlawed, for reasons none of them clearly understood. Their old captain had been a man they respected and admired, and they had served him well. Marquet was neither—but he was feared, and so they obeyed him equally well. But as their lives and the lives of everyone in Aquila grew harsher under Marquet's heel, the guardsmen muttered blackly that someday their former captain would return and claim his revenge. Marquet heard the whispers; and, fearing the same thing, only grew uglier-tempered.

Now Marquet looked up at the gallows, smiling in satisfaction at the swinging bodies—three wretches who had been caught stealing grain from the Bishop's storehouses. On his helmet golden eagle wings, the symbol of his rank, winked in the sunlight as he nodded. "That should give them a bellyful," he murmured. The Bishop had made him captain because he could be counted on to carry out the Bishop's orders unflinchingly . . . and to enjoy his work. He turned back to his lieutenant. "Jehan! The next three."

Jehan saluted and led his men away across the stone-paved square toward the dungeons of Aquila Castle. Entering an underground passage, they circled down and down the narrow, slippery steps cut out of solid rock—the single, heavily guarded entrance to a prison they had come to know far too well in recent months. The air grew danker and fouler as they descended, and they began to hear the moaning of the prisoners down below.

The dungeons lay in a vast hole carved from the bedrock on which the castle sat, as deep and inescapable as the pits of hell. A gridwork of wood and iron divided the chamber into a honeycomb of countless cells and cages, all with a clear view of the dungeons' instruments of torture. Jehan shouted as the guardsmen reached bottom. The head jailer came lumbering toward them with a torch in his hand, a ring of iron keys jangling at his belt. "Why don't you build a bigger gibbet?" he growled. "Save me some bother down here."

"At least you're just visiting," one of the guards said. He held his nose. Jehan snorted. The jailer led them along scaffolded corridors past cell after cell. The moans and cries died away as they passed; ghostly faces shrank back from the mold-slick bars. The prisoners cowered in the darkness, still believing there was something worse than the living death in which they now existed.

Jehan stopped before a cell in the deepest recesses of the pit and peered through the grate, searching with sudden eagerness for the gallows' next victim. He remembered this particular prisoner; he had heaved him into the cell personally. The young thief who was about to hang had made fools of the Guard for months, eluding them time after time, before they had finally captured him. Jehan looked forward to watching the slippery little rat swing.

Jehan stared through the lattice of bars. It

took his eyes a long moment of blinking to adjust to the gloom on the other side. He held his breath; the stench of human waste and sickness was overwhelming. As his eyes adjusted, he made out two ragged figures propped against the far wall. One of them stared fixedly ahead, as if his mind had fled this hellhole, leaving his body behind. The other prisoner hummed a tuneless song, murmuring unintelligibly under his breath. Even in the darkness, he knew that neither of their gaunt, filthy faces was the one he wanted. He pressed against the bars, searching every corner of the cell. There was no one else in it. "Phillipe Gaston?" he said, puzzled. He turned to the jailer. "Wrong cell. I want Phillipe Gaston, the one they call the Mouse."

The mumbling prisoner began to sing audibly, "The mouse, the mouse . . . has left our house . . ."

The jailer held up his torch and peered at the almost unreadable scratches on the cell door. "One thirty-two, sir. This is it."

"He's run away," the prisoner sang, "no mouse today . . ." He giggled, gesturing across the cell with a bony hand.

Jehan pressed against the bars again, looking harder into the shadowed corners of the cell. This time he saw the open drainage grate. Jehan gaped in disbelief. The hole was no more than one foot square—surely no adult human being, not even that scrawny, half-grown wretch Gaston, could have escaped through it. As he watched, a small rat scurried up out of the hole and across the reeking cell floor.

". . . to stop the pain, he's down the drain . . ."

"Shut up, you idiot!" Jehan snarled. He looked back at the jailer. "Open the door!"

The jailer fumbled with his keys, unlocking the door with frantic haste. Jehan and the guards pushed into the cell. "What happened to him?" Jehan demanded roughly.

The singer gazed up at him with mindless calm. "I just told you, gentle lord." He gestured at the drain hole. "I tried to escape myself, but I couldn't fit." He smiled, holding up his hands. "So since he still lives, you can kill me twice."

Jehan turned away, seeing nothing but the face of Phillipe Gaston, who was not there. He shoved his guardsmen toward the door furiously. "Search every sewer! Every drain! Find him, or Captain Marquet will hang you in his place!" *And maybe me too, damn him.* He listened to their frightened footsteps retreating down the hall. He glanced one last time at the drain hole. "Incredible," he muttered. With a curse of frustration, he left the cell.

Chapter Two

Far beneath Aquila Castle the drain hole opened
on another world—a world even more forbidding than the castle dungeons. The sewers of
Aquila had begun with the town in Roman
times, as the skilled engineers of the Empire
took advantage of a natural system of caverns
lying beneath the early settlement for drainage
and waste disposal. Once the sewers had been
part of an orderly, structured plan, like the city
itself. But they had been left to fester and de-
cay through the centuries since the Empire's
fall, as the city had spread out over the plain
above them in a completely random and uncon-
trolled way. Now they were an unfathomable
maze wormholing the underground beneath every building and street—another world, but one

which no sane citizen of Aquila had any desire
to enter.

That secret, subterranean world lay waiting
in eternal silence, disturbed only by the occasional squeaking of rats, the drip of effluence,
and the distant rushing of water. But now its
dark peace was broken by new and unexpected
sounds. The grunts and gasps and scraping
noises were faint at first, but they grew louder,
until they echoed from the drainage hole into
the empty tunnel below. Suddenly an arm thrust
out of the hole into the open air. It waved
wildly up and down, in astonishment and
triumph. After the arm came part of a shoulder.
Then the rest of the lithe, small-boned body of
Phillipe Gaston emerged, piece by piece, like a
newborn child. Wriggling and twisting like an
acrobat, the young thief dragged himself free of
the drain at last and dropped to the floor.

He sat gasping for breath, hardly noticing the
stench as he filled his lungs completely for the
first time in far too long. He looked back at the
hole with a kind of disbelief, and a small
crooked smile pulled at his mouth. "Not unlike
escaping Mother's womb, really," he murmured.
"God, what a memory. . . ." He looked away
again, shuddering. His skin was scraped raw,
the rags of his clothing were slimy with filth.
His fingernails were torn and bloody from claw-
ing his way down the drain. It had taken him
hours to force his body through, hours that had
seemed like years. The drainhole had not

dropped straight into the sewer, but had doubled back on itself like a snake. Time after time he had thought he was hopelessly trapped in some elbow or coil of its intestines. But he had no other choice except to keep on struggling, and in the end he had won free. He had escaped from the dungeons, and the good citizens of Aquila would never see him again . . . if he could just find his way out of their sewers.

He crouched where he was, slowly looking around. The immensity of this underground world awed him. He had often been in cities the size of Aquila, but he had never been in the sewers of one; in most of the cities he had seen, the sewers simply ran down the middle of the street. At least the darkness was not complete—dim light shafted down through countless drain openings from the world above. His eyes, used to the gloom of the dungeons, had no trouble seeing.

The first thing he saw was a human skeleton, embedded in the black sludge an arm's length away. He jerked back with a startled cry. The yellowed skull grinned in empty mirth. He answered it with a rueful grin of his own, and studied the skeleton speculatively. "Six foot two, eh?" His voice rang dimly in the tunnel. He stood up, stretching his own small body to its full height. "An ideal height for passing through the gates of heaven, my friend. But you see where our Lord in His infinite wisdom has chosen to deposit us." He gestured around him, looked up at the dripping ceiling suddenly. "I'm not complaining, mind you," he called out to heaven. "Just ... pointing things out." He shrugged. He had what he liked to think of as a personal relationship with God; it was a comfort to know that the Lord was always listening to him, even if no one else ever did. He didn't want to seem ungrateful when his prayers were answered, even by this mixed blessing. He sighed and began to walk, his feet squelching in the ooze.

Far above him, but not as far above as heaven, the Bishop's Guard were filling the streets of Aquila in search of their escaped prisoner. A squad entered the belfry of the cathedral at Marquet's order and pulled the heavy bell ropes. For the first time in years, the cathedral's enormous bells sounded an alarm through the city.

Within the cathedral, Mass still continued. But as the bells pealed out, filling the vast hall with their sound, the worshipers looked at each other in astonishment and fright. The Bishop turned away from the altar, his impassive face suddenly taut with concern. He glanced over the heads of the standing crowd and saw Marquet. The Captain of the Guard stood near the rear of the cathedral, in the doorway to a private chapel. The golden wings on his helmet flashed in the light as he nodded urgently.

The Bishop went on with the Mass, his singsong recitation more ominous than before.

* * *

Down below, Phillipe the Mouse crept through the sewer caverns like his namesake, crouching low until his back ached as he squeezed through a narrow passage into another vast subterranean chamber. He straightened up at last, out of breath, his back muscles pinched in a spasm. Grimacing, he wiped his filthy face on his filthy sleeve and squinted back the way he had come, then ahead again. He saw nothing but the same patternless maze of treacherous tunnels and caves, the same black, reeking pools and streamers of fungus stretching to infinity. For a moment the thought struck him that he might actually have died, and gone to hell.

He shook his head, shaking droplets of water and slime from his sodden hair. No . . . he was too miserable to be dead. He was still alive—but he wondered suddenly how long he would have to go on like this. Panic squeezed his chest as it occurred to him that he might never find his way out of this underground tomb; that he might wander here, alone and lost, until he died.

He sat down in the mud, wracked with sudden shivers. "Easy does it, Mouse," he murmured softly, clenching his fists. He forced himself to take a deep breath, and another. "Steady progress . . . a peaceful Sunday walk through the gardens . . ." He pushed his mind into the hidden world of his daydreams, blocking out the endless maze of caverns, the terror of being lost in their darkness. He had always been too small, too weak, or too poor; his imagination was the one thing he counted on for survival, and the only refuge he had from reality. At last, almost calm again, he got to his feet and waded back into the oily, knee-deep water, letting his mind lead him on through his Sunday stroll.

Hours passed, as Phillipe wandered through the underworld; his fear settled slowly into weary resignation. He picked his way precariously along a ledge high on a cavern wall, edging around another outcrop of stone—and found himself eye to eye with a screeching demon. He shouted and flung himself backward, recognizing it, too late, as the face of a yowling cat. The cat hissed and bounded off into the darkness. His own feet turned him around and sent him stumbling away in the other direction. Looking back as he ran, he felt the ledge drop out from under him with a sudden, sickening rush. The mud-caked edge of the shelf had broken away beneath his feet.

He plunged his fingers into the slimy earth of the wall as he fell, and dug in desperately. After a moment of blinding panic his eyes began to focus again, as he realized he was not still falling. For the first time he really became aware of the rushing noise that filled the vast tunnel, the sound of a great river flowing past somewhere in the darkness. Barely daring to

breathe, he looked down past his dangling feet.
And down and down.

Below him he watched the black waters of
the subterranean river roar by. Dim light falling from somewhere above showed him the
enormous bleached skull of a cow, caught in
the sludge on its shore. Long, slimy eels darted
in and out of the skull's empty eyesockets.

Phillipe shut his own eyes with a small moan.
"Lord," he whispered, "*I will never pick another pocket again as long as I live, I swear.*"
His voice trembled slightly. "But . . . here's the
problem: If You don't let me live, how can I
prove my good faith to You?" There was no
answer. Phillipe looked up; water dripped into
his eye. "I'm going to pull myself up now,
Lord," he said, more firmly. His fingers were
beginning to cramp. Still no answer. "If You've
heard me this shelf will remain steady as a
rock. If not, then no hard feelings, of course.
But I will be *very* disappointed."

Gritting his teeth, he kicked a foothold in the
wall, and then another. He pulled one hand
free of the muck, dug it in again, nearer to the
broken ledge. The earth held. Inch by miracu-
lous inch, he clawed his way back to the shelf,
and dragged himself painfully up onto it. He
flopped down on its solid surface and shook
out his arms and legs, amazed to find his body
still in one piece. "I don't believe it." He shook
his head, getting cautiously to his feet.

Suddenly organ music filled the air around

him. Phillipe looked up, awestruck. Above him a long shaft opened, snaking its way upward toward a glowing light. Phillipe sank to his knees, transfixed, as the music and light enfolded him. "I *believe* it," he whispered hoarsely. Not wanting to keep the Lord waiting, he got to his feet again and scrambled up into the shaft.

The way to heaven was not an easy one. It was crooked and steep and slippery. Filthy water dripped into his eyes from cracks in the rockface. The corroded iron rungs that gave him hand- and footholds seemed to have been there for as long as the stone. Halfway to the top, one gave way suddenly under his weight, and sent him sliding back down toward the darkness. He jammed his foot frantically into another rung. It groaned in protest, but it held.

Phillipe looked up again, breathing hard. The light was stronger now above him, and the organ music was deafening. A choir began to sing. He began to climb again, filled with fresh inspiration. He reached the top of the shaft at last and lifted his head eagerly. His eyes widened.

Above him, a heavy iron grating blocked the entrance of the shaft. And through it, high above, he saw a radiant vision of night-black and blinding brightness. He shut his eyes, opened them again. The vision of night and day resolved itself into the luminous colors and intricate patterns of a circular stained-glass window.

Phillipe hung onto the grating and stared. He knew that window . . . it was the rose window above the entrance of the Aquila Cathedral. The window was all he could see, but now he knew that Sunday Mass was what he had heard . . . and Mass would make the perfect cover for his escape. The Lord had been listening to him after all. He wedged himself against the shaft walls and began to push upward on the grating.

Two paces in front of him, hidden from his sight by the angle of the drain, stood the heavy boots and thick uniformed back of the Captain of the Guard. Marquet frowned, waiting impatiently in the vestry for Mass to end.

A raggedly dressed family stood near him, singing along with the choir and stealing occasional uneasy glances in his direction. Their little girl, bored and restless from standing for hours at the edge of the crowd, stared at him openly. Her wandering eyes found the grate in the floor behind him next; she watched in amazement as fingers emerged through its cracks and danced in the air. The grate began to twitch and jump. The little girl grinned and giggled. Her father hushed her. "Papa—!" She pointed, tugging at his hand.

Marquet looked idly at her, glanced back over his shoulder. Her father jerked her around again to face the altar. Marquet turned and looked into the chapel, his curiosity mingling with suspicion. He took a step into the room, and then another.

The choir burst into an ecstatic salvo as his heavy military boot came down on the grate, crushing Phillipe's exposed fingers. Phillipe's scream of pain was drowned in music as he fell back down the shaft.

He slid and bounced dizzily downward, his flailing arms reaching wildly for any handhold. Suddenly his fingers closed over more fingers— another human hand. He clung to it, pulling hard. It snapped from the rotting arm of a buried corpse, and he screamed again as he fell on down the shaft.

He crashed down onto the slick, muddy sewer shelf. Before he could stop himself, his momentum had carried him on over the edge. He plummeted sickeningly through the air, and the raging black waters of the river rose up to meet him.

He plunged into the river, sinking deep, choking on the foul water. He fought his way back to the surface, spitting and gagging. The current swept him along as he floundered helplessly in a sea of loathsome debris. A dead rat draped itself around his throat, a horse's head banged against his own, a dozen more unrecognizable horrors swirled past him. Dazed and battered, half drowned, he struggled to stay afloat.

Abruptly his body smashed into something hard and unyielding that stopped his motion downstream. Blinking the water out of his eyes, he found himself up against an iron grille clogged with centuries of sodden refuse. He hung on to the bars, coughing and wheezing, until a sudden rush of comprehension cleared his head. There could be only one reason why a grille would be barring his way ... he had reached the city walls. He looked up, saw faint rays of daylight seeping through the refuse-clogged iron bars that were the last obstacle separating him from freedom. High above him, the grille was lodged solidly in the stone roof of the outlet. The only way past it was down ... if there was a way past it.

He clung to the bars a moment longer, gathering his courage. Then, taking as deep a breath as his waterlogged lungs would hold, he dove under the surface. The surging current caught him in its wild grip, sweeping him down beneath a dam of submerged debris. The rushing water pinned him there, trapped against the bottom of the grill, in spite of his panic-stricken struggles. He groped frantically through the darkness along the spikes at the bottom of the bars, his lungs aching, his mind beginning to grow dim and fuzzy. Suddenly he felt empty space— an opening, not wide enough for a normal man, but more than large enough for Phillipe the Mouse. He dragged himself under the grille and shot upward through the brightening water.

His head broke the water's surface in the light of day. He sucked in a huge, ragged gasp of fresh air, another and another, as he stared up at the high, forbidding walls of Aquila from the outside. He was in the moat. He was free at last.

He heard the warning bells still pealing through the town, the sounds of shouting guardsmen and horses galloping past the city gate. He was free . . . but he wasn't safe. Squinting in the sunlight, he looked across the moat and the flat, open fields beyond, toward the sanctuary of the distant hills. He sighed in resignation and began to drift silently out into the moat.

Far up in the hills, too far away to make out any clear detail of the city, the rider in black sat listening to the unexpected sound of the alarm bells. He gazed down at the city for a long while; and then, as if he had reached some decision, he reined his black stallion around and started down the hillside toward Aquila. In another moment he was lost from sight among the reds and golds of the autumn trees.

Chapter Three

The Bishop moved serenely through the atrium courtyard of Castle Aquila, his exquisite and heavily guarded personal domain. Chrysanthemums and roses still bloomed in the court's green and sheltered gardens, giving the impression, as he did, that life was perfectly ordered and completely under control. His personal bodyguard and secretary followed him at a discreet distance, as they always did. Outside his private chambers he was constantly on display, and long experience had taught him never to show anything to anyone.

He glanced up as the sound of booted feet intruded on his not-so-peaceful contemplation. Captain Marquet was hurrying toward him through the gardens. The Bishop's mouth tightened. He had not forgotten for an instant the sound of alarm bells interrupting the Mass. But he would not let even Marquet sense his concern. The exercise of complete power demanded at least the appearance of complete confidence.

"Alarming news, Your Grace—" Marquet burst out, halting breathlessly before him.

The Bishop frowned. "You forget yourself, Marquet."

Marquet's face froze. He dropped to his knees instantly, in reflex, and kissed the emerald ring that the Bishop held out to him. But before he had risen to his feet again, the fatal words slipped out: "One of the prisoners has escaped."

The Bishop jerked his hand away, his pale eyes glittering. "No one escapes the dungeons of Aquila," he said softly. "The people of this city accept that as a matter of historical fact."

Marquet swallowed. "The responsibility is mine," he murmured. Sweat stood out on his brow.

"Yes."

Marquet dared to glance up again. "It would be a miracle if he made it through the sewage system—"

"I believe in miracles, Marquet," the Bishop said. "They are an unshakable component of my faith."

Marquet looked away nervously. "At any rate . . ." He fumbled for the words that would lift the sword of the Bishop's displeasure from his neck. "It's only one insignificant petty thief . . . a nameless piece of human garbage . . ."

The Bishop stared coldly at him. "Great storms announce themselves with a simple breeze, Captain. And the fires of rebellion can be ignited by a single random spark." He looked away, his eyes growing distant, as if he possessed some otherworldly knowledge, given to him in a way that no ordinary mortal could comprehend.

Marquet rose to his feet, his jaw set. "If he's out there, I'll find him, Your Grace!"

The Bishop looked back at his captain, and his eyes narrowed. "Since you have my blessing, I can only envy your inevitable success in the matter."

Marquet bobbed his head like a chastened schoolboy, no longer able even to meet the gaze of the blinding figure in white who stood before him. He knew better than most men that the Bishop did not hold his position of power by the simple grace of God . . . He turned on his heel and walked away as quickly as he dared.

The Bishop watched him go. Only when Marquet was almost out of sight did the Bishop's eyelids suddenly twitch with unreadable apprehension. He fingered his emerald ring, twisting it on his hand.

Marquet mounted his horse and rode away from his audience at the castle as if devils were on his tail. His men had searched the city and its sewers, and found nothing. Surely that filthy little maggot Phillipe Gaston must be dead. But just in case he was not, Marquet called his men together to search the surrounding countryside as well.

At the base of the curving bridge by the city gates, guardsmen gathered on horseback around an oxcart loaded with supplies. Marquet turned impatiently in his saddle as his second-in-command, Jehan, rode up. "Take ten men toward Chenet!" he shouted. "I'll ride north to Gavroche." Already the sun was setting; there would be little time left to search before nightfall. More horsemen milled around him as he issued orders. He stood in his stirrups to locate the supply cart, spurred his horse toward it.

And behind him, a small dripping shadow darted out from beneath the bridge's arch and scuttled under the legs of the milling horses.

"You!" Marquet shouted to the two men on the supply cart. "Take the supplies." The shadow passed under the supply cart as Marquet rode up alongside it, and suddenly disappeared. "We'll rendezvous outside the gates of Gavroche at noon tomorrow." Marquet looked back at his waiting troops, his eyes hard. "The name of the man who finds Phillipe Gaston will be brought to the personal attention of the Bishop! As will the body—of the man who lets him get away." He watched as Jehan rode off at a gallop with his troops, stones and sparks flying from beneath their horses' hooves. Then he jerked his

own horse's head around and led his men away
to the north.

The two guards left behind with the supply
cart looked at each other in the empty silence
that followed, and shrugged. The driver cracked
his whip. The oxen lumbered forward, pulling
the creaky wooden cart away down the rutted
road.

Wedged between the oxcart's wheels, Phillipe
clung to its mud-spattered underside like a burr,
with his feet jammed into the rear corner joints.
He smiled, and winced, as the cart began to
move at last; he groped with his abused fingers
for a better handhold. A loose board in the
bottom of the cart gave unexpectedly as he
pushed against it. He grinned and slid the board
aside, never one to ignore the potential of a
situation. Pushing his arm up through the
opening, he let his hand roam by feel among
the supplies.

His heart leaped as his fingers closed over
something he recognized instantly and unmis-
takably: the pouch full of coins hanging from
the driver's belt. Ever so gently, he tugged on
the strings.

"We're looking for a ghost, if you ask me,"
the voice of the second guard said sullenly.

Phillipe hesitated, then tugged again on the
purse. Its strings were knotted too firmly. His
hand made a fist in frustration, began to grope
farther along the belt.

"Careful—" the driver said; Phillipe's hand

froze. "They say the Bishop leaves his window open at night, and the voices of discontent are brought to him on a black cloud."

Phillipe's fingers brushed the driver's dagger, hanging next to the money pouch. He slid it from its sheath with a skill born of long practice, and slit the purse strings deftly. The money purse and the dagger disappeared through the floorboards without a sound.

"In that case," the second guard said, "I have a message for the Bishop." He farted loudly. "Close your window!" The two men guffawed with laughter.

Beneath the cart, Phillipe pulled open the pouch and examined its contents with a shrewd eye. He smiled; glanced up with sudden guilt at the sliver of sky shining down through the boards. "I know I promised, Lord," he whispered. "Never again. But I also know You realize what a weak-willed person I am. This is Your way of pointing that out to me, and I humbly accept my punishment in Your name." Pulling his feet from the corners of the wagon and letting go with his hands, he dropped silently out from under the wheels into the dusty road. The cart and its occupants rumbled on, oblivious, into the twilight.

Phillipe got to his knees in time to see the last rays of the setting sun disappear behind the distant hills. Somewhere close by, a wolf howled. The desolate, haunted sound echoed across the empty land. Phillipe looked up with a shudder, and crept away into the bushes at the side of the road.

For the next two days Phillipe lived the life of a hunted animal. The guardsmen of Aquila swarmed everywhere, covering the countryside like a plague of vermin, promising rich rewards for his capture and ruthless punishment for anyone who gave him aid. The fury and the thoroughness of their search astonished and dismayed him. The idea that they would go to so much trouble to catch one insignificant pickpocket was more than he could comprehend. But he did not dare to show his face at so much as a peasant's hovel while they were still searching, and so he survived on roots and berries and half-rotten leavings from the fields. He had a pouch full of coins hidden under his rags, but he had not been able to get close enough to a house even to steal food or clothing. By day he hid in the forest; at night he slept in trees to avoid the equally pitiless hunters of the dark.

Even the weather seemed to turn against him. The sky that had remained nearly cloudless for two years, in spite of the farmers' endless prayers, suddenly filled with storm clouds, sending down torrents of rain driven by the cold autumn wind. Phillipe spent his second hungry, freezing night in the woods huddled in the crook of an ancient tree, beneath a hopelessly inadequate shelter woven of branches. Clinging

to the trunk with numb hands while the relentless rain poured down his face, he gnawed on a
shriveled turnip until his stomach knotted and
rebelled. He threw the half-eaten remains down
out of the tree in disgust. Resting his head
against the rough bark of the trunk, he closed
his eyes, his misery complete. Somewhere there
must be a better world than this one . . . and if
he only believed in it enough, he could be
there. . . . He set his mind free into the un-
charted lands of his imagination. His eyes
squeezed shut, water dripping from his lashes
and his nose, and he slowly began to smile.

Somewhere in the land of his dreams the sun
was shining, as it always was, warmly on his
back. "It's summer," he murmured, with a sigh.
"The bright hot sun dances like a child on the
blue water. And . . . she appears." He saw her
clearly now, her hair more dazzling than the
sun, her fair young face more beautiful than
the roses and lilies beside the lake. His heart
filled with joy as she kissed him tenderly and
vowed that she would never leave him. "Oh,
Phillipe, I love you so . . . I never knew a
moment's happiness but for you. . . ."

In the morning, when he woke, he discovered that the weather, at least, had relented.
His hopes brightened with the sunrise. He
climbed down from the tree, moving like an
arthritic old man. Stretching the cramps from

his arms and legs, he ate a handful of squashed berries and started away through the woods.

The morning was sunny, and warm for fall. His clothes dried out for the first time in days. Around noontime he was finally able to creep up close enough to a solitary cottage to steal a loaf of bread that had been left to cool on a window shelf. He didn't stop to say a grace before he devoured it, hoping that the Lord would recognize his gratitude by the speed with which it disappeared.

Strengthened by his first substantial meal in longer than he could remember, he moved on toward the hills. He had not seen any guardsmen all morning, and he began to hope that he had outdistanced or at least outwaited them. Surely they must have given up hunting a single worthless thief by now. He would not feel slighted in the least if they had.

Late in the afternoon he dared to stop beside a small river to rest and clean himself up. The pouring rain had already washed away the most repulsive part of the filth and stench he had brought with him out of the city. *A cloud with a small silver lining*, he thought, not as grateful as he might have been. His tunic and pants, which had been old and worn to begin with, were in rags now; but so were many people's, these days. And with luck, he could steal some better ones. If he could make himself halfway presentable, with the coins in his money pouch he could pass for an honest traveler and not a hunted fugitive. He pictured himself eating good hot stew, drinking mulled wine until his wits were numb, sleeping in the warm bed of an inn tonight instead of a tree ... he smiled contentedly.

He settled down on a warm rock, half hidden among the weeds and rushes of the riverside. He rubbed his aching feet, savoring the view of the setting sun framed in the bridge's arch. Then, very carefully, he stripped off his ruined shirt, grimacing as the coarse cloth scraped the angry, half-healed welts on his back. He reached around and touched them gingerly, wincing. Before his capture, he had led the Bishop's Guard on a wild and furious chase through Aquila's maze of streets. But they had caught him in the end, and had beaten him thoroughly in retribution.

He threw his shirt down, some of his good mood fading. "You've sent them all against me, Lord," he said, lifting his chin, taking a certain stubborn pride in his martyrdom. "But still I survive. You see before you a modern-day Job. . . ." He splashed his face with icy river water, gasping with the cold as he scrubbed his skin with his hands.

He watched his reflection emerge for the better in the gleaming mirror of the water. His clean face smiled back at him from under an unkempt thatch of dark brown hair—really rather a handsome face, he thought. A little too thin, of course ... but then, considering the

manner of his recent escape from the dungeons,
he supposed he should be grateful that he hadn't
been overfed these last few weeks. He ran a
hand that was still covered with green-and-
purple bruises along his smooth cheek. The
features of his face were quite sensitive and
refined, actually ... they suited the face of a
noble's son who had been stolen away at birth
by treacherous enemies and raised by humble
peasants as their own. His father, the Duke,
had no idea that his long-lost heir still lived,
and so he had never bothered to search for
him. But someday they would meet, and the
father would recognize his son instantly from
the incredible resemblance between them. . . .

The lost lord's dark eyes widened as a sudden noise above and behind him startled him
back into reality. Phillipe spun around, grabbing his shirt, looking up the hillside. Far above,
two horsemen in the unmistakable crimson uniforms of the Bishop's Guard were riding down
the hill toward the river's edge. He took a deep
breath and leaped into the water.

Jehan and a second guardsman rode down to
the river through the tall, ripened grasses. Jehan
beat at the reeds by the waterside with the flat
of his sword; he searched the surrounding countryside with weary eyes and rising frustration.
"I could swear I saw somebody—!" He sat back,
dropping his reins, and sheathed his sword.

The second guardsman shifted restlessly in

his saddle, without finding a soft spot. "How much longer, sir?" His horse moved forward and began to graze beside Jehan's, yanking up tufts of tender young rushes at the water's edge.

"Until Captain Marquet has been satisfied— that the Bishop has been satisfied," Jehan said truculently.

Their barely intelligible voices carried dimly to Phillipe, lying on his back beneath the water's surface among the rushes. He breathed shallowly through the hollow stalk of a reed, watching foam from the mouths of the grazing horses drift lazily downward toward his face. *Why me, Lord?* he thought.

And then the reed was jerked abruptly from between his teeth. A horse had torn it free, along with a mouthful of rushes. Suddenly breathless, Phillipe barely stopped the gasp of shock that would have drowned him. He clutched frantically at the rushes, holding himself down against his frenzied need to leap up and fill his lungs with air.

"Marquet's life hangs in the balance," Jehan droned somewhere up above, "and he knows it."

Leave! Leave! Phillipe's mind screamed. Any minute his lungs would burst . . . any second—

Jehan's horse plunged its nose into the water again, rooting among the weeds. All at once a violent spout of spray exploded into its face. The horse lunged backward with a snort of panic, nearly throwing Jehan into the river.

Jehan pulled leather frantically, saving himself
from a fall. Getting his mount under control, he
turned back to the water's edge.

Before his astonished eyes there suddenly
stood the equally astonished figure of Phillipe
Gaston. Jehan stared, his face filling with recognition and rage.

"I'm sorry," Phillipe gasped, not quite ration-
ally. "That's entirely my fault. Here, let me dry
your horse off. . . ." He stumbled toward the
shore in a daze of fear.

"It's him!" the second guard shouted.

"No, it's not!" Phillipe shrieked.

Jehan's sword was already in his hand. "Get
him!"

Phillipe turned to dive back into the river,
but the other guard was there before him, cutting him off, driving him back to the shore. As
he scrambled up the bank, Jehan bore down on
him, the guardsman's sword shining and deadly
in his hand. Phillipe yelled hysterically as the
blade came down to cut him in two. But instead its flat struck him hard on the rump and
knocked him sprawling in the grass. He rolled
onto his back, looking up in disbelief. Jehan's
face loomed above him, grinning savagely. Then
he understood: They were playing a game of
cat and mouse. . . .

Phillipe scrambled to his feet and bolted up
the hill, running harder than he had ever run.
Above him was the bridge; if he could only get
to the bridge . . .

The two horsemen followed him at an easy canter, letting him run himself out. Their laughter goaded him like a lash.

He reached the top of the hill at last, just as he had decided it was endless. Sobbing for air, he threw himself onto the bridge and began to run across it. The flat wooden planks gave him fresh speed; but behind him he heard the clatter of hooves burst onto the wood. He looked back, futilely, as he ran, and his foot caught on a loose board. He pitched forward onto the hard planks, knocking the last of his breath out of him. He lay still for a long moment, paralyzed by the knowledge of his imminent death. But no sword fell, no blinding instant of pain ended his terror. An uncanny silence stretched on and on around him, until finally he dared to raise his head. His jaw dropped.

His head rested between the steel-shod hooves and muscular forelegs of an enormous black war-horse. The hooves shifted slightly; wisps of steam curled from the great beast's nostrils into the chill air. Dark eyes rolled to look down at him with almost human suspicion from its finely formed head. The horse was the most magnificent creature he had ever seen. And then he saw the black-clad leg of a rider pressing its side.

Phillipe pushed himself up slowly, jerked upright as the fierce, golden-eyed hawk resting on the rider's gauntlet screamed suddenly. It hissed at him, flaring its wings. Phillipe sat back on his knees, gaping at the man who controlled both hawk and horse. The looming, hooded figure, dressed all in black, could only be the Fifth Horseman of the Apocalypse. His black cloak was lined with flaming red, like a glimpse of hellfire as he shifted in his saddle to look down at Phillipe. He held a gleaming broadsword in his free hand, and the cold blue eyes that shone in his shadowed face were as distant and threatening as the land of Death. Phillipe tore his gaze away from the silent figure and looked back over his shoulder.

The two guardsmen sat on their horses, momentarily frozen with the same awe. Their mounts pranced and backed nervously, as if even they sensed the aura of danger that hung about the man in black.

At last Jehan roused himself and said, "Clear the bridge."

The stranger made no reply, sitting motionless on his horse. The rising wind moaned uneasily in the trees.

"The man's an escaped prisoner." Jehan raised his voice. "We're taking him in."

"On whose authority?" the stranger asked at last.

"His Grace, the Bishop of Aquila."

Only Phillipe saw the fleeting, involuntary twitch of the stranger's mouth that might have been a smile. And then the war-horse lunged forward, the hawk rose shrieking into the air.

Phillipe threw himself aside, barely avoiding being trampled.

The second guard charged forward to meet the man in black, his sword raised. The stranger's horse reared, with all the fury and splendor of a mythological beast. One deadly sweep of the stranger's sword cut through the guardsman's ribcage, sent him sideways off his horse and over the edge of the bridge. His scream echoed as he plummeted toward the river below.

Before the first man struck the water, the stranger had turned on Jehan, unhorsing him in one swift motion. Jehan crumpled to the planks of the bridge; he tried to rise again, only to find the stranger standing over him with his sword point jammed at his throat. Jehan swallowed hard, looking up with white-ringed eyes into the face of Death.

The man in black pushed back his hood. Jehan's face turned even paler as he recognized the man who stood over him. "Return to Marquet," the stranger said. "Tell him Navarre is back."

Jehan nodded, speechless with fear. He got to his feet and ran back the way he had come. The man called Navarre stood watching as Jehan mounted his horse and galloped away into the dusk. At last the stranger turned back and remounted his own horse. The hawk spiraled down out of the indigo heights of the sky and settled on his wrist again. He sat for a moment, gazing curiously at Phillipe, who still stood weak-kneed with awe where he had left him. Then he nudged his horse forward, riding toward the small, silent, waiting figure.

Phillipe shook himself out of his daze, pulling himself up until he was almost standing on his toes. "Magnificent, sir!" he shouted. "A dazzling display! As I'm sure you could tell, I was in the process of luring them onto the bridge when you arrived, and . . ."

Navarre reined in his horse, staring down at Phillipe with a cryptic smile. "An escaped prisoner from Aquila?" he said, almost to himself. "Not from the dungeons."

"Why not from the dungeons?" Phillipe asked.

"No one ever has." The man spoke the words like someone who knew why it ought to be impossible.

Phillipe raised his eyebrows, considering the possibility that he had actually done something remarkable. But he only shrugged, too much of a gentleman to brag about his exploits.

Navarre leaned forward across his saddlebow, studying Phillipe thoughtfully. Then all at once he looked up again, away toward the west, where the sun was disappearing behind the hills. His face turned grim and tight. Prodding his mount with his spurs, Navarre started on across the bridge, passing Phillipe silently, as if he had ceased to exist.

Startled, Phillipe reached up, not quite daring to put a hand on the other man. "Sir? Wait. . . ." Navarre did not even glance down.

Phillipe trotted after him, calling out, "You see, the truth is I've been thinking of taking on a traveling companion. . . ." Still no response. More desperately, he shouted, "There are more guards out there! You'll need a good man to watch your flank!" He was running.

The stranger rode away into the darkness without looking back.

Phillipe stopped running, letting his hands drop. He glanced down at himself. "Oh, shut up, Mouse," he muttered. He turned around and walked back to the bridge, trying to ignore the nameless ache that was suddenly filling his chest. He peered down past the edge of the wooden planks, seeing the body of the dead guard drifting in the reeds. He shook his head ruefully. "You were severely outclassed, my friend. You never had a chance." He glanced back in the direction the stranger had gone, with a brief smile of gratitude and regret. And then he went on across the bridge to the guard's waiting horse, to unhook the purse from its saddle. "It is easier for a camel to pass through the eye of a needle than for a rich man to enter the Kingdom of Heaven." He glanced back at the body. "Don't mention it," he called, as he started on his way again.

Chapter Four

During the midnight hours the rain returned with a vengeance. Phillipe wondered dismally whether two years of drought had really come to an end just to make his life miserable. He spent another wretched night in a tree, startled awake out of dreams of a magnificent warrior in black by flashes of lightning and the rumble of thunder. Once he would even have sworn that it was a horse's scream which woke him; that he saw the mighty black rear up on a distant hilltop—riderless—and disappear into the storm.

But by dawn none of it was more than the fading memory of a nightmare. Phillipe dropped to the ground and set out again, moving upslope. He was in the foothills now, where he hoped he could safely elude the Bishop's pursuit at last. He scrambled up and down the muddy hills of the roughening terrain, picking his way through russet-colored brush and the slippery yellow leaves of the oak forest. Even here he kept one part of his mind always alert for any sign of horsemen. The fact that he now knew why the Bishop's guards were so determined to recapture him did not make him any more willing to give them the chance. But in spite of his caution, he never saw the rider in black reappear on a ridge behind him shortly after dawn; never realized that the stranger followed him all through the morning.

At last Phillipe reached a small village nestled in a narrow mountain valley. The farming here was even poorer than in the drought-stricken plain around Aquila. The dismal warren of mudbrick-and-plaster houses that squatted inside a crumbling stone wall was proof enough of the poverty of the villagers' lives. But Phillipe, crouched shivering behind a ramshackle shed just inside the walls, observed that they were still better off than he was. It was shortly after noon, and few of the villagers seemed to be in sight. He supposed they must be in their homes, warm and dry, eating their midday meals. . . . The thought of food made his throat ache. If no one else was outside, miserable and starving, then now was the perfect time to get himself some decent clothes. "It is more blessed to give than to receive," he muttered, and darted out of hiding to snatch a pair of boots left to dry on a doorstep.

Safely back under cover, he pulled off the ruins of his soft-soled shoes and pushed his feet into the damp leather of the boots, wrapping the bindings tightly around his legs to keep them on. He stood up, grinning with satisfaction. He was Phillipe the Mouse, the only man who had ever escaped from the dungeons of Aquila. For him, this was child's play. Quickly he visited another yard, yanking a hooded woolen tunic from a clothesline, rejecting a pair of pants nearly as ragged as his own.

The tunic engulfed him like a shroud as he pulled it on. Rolling the sleeves up until his hands were free, he made his way on around the edge of the village. Behind a house that was either under construction or collapsing, he found another clothesline with a better-preserved pair of pants on it. He crept into the yard, straightened briefly to inspect them at close range. He made a face. "His tailor could be a better friend to him, but . . ." Shrugging, he jerked the pants from the line. He glanced away suddenly, as he caught the odor of food and woodsmoke in the air. Between the houses he spotted a sagging tavern. Smoke wafted from its chimney. Barely stopping long enough to change his pants, he hurried down the muddy street.

Villagers sat outside the dark tavern entrance, enjoying the last of the outdoor half of the year.

They ate and drank at wooden tables beneath the shelter of a vine-hung lattice in the squalid yard. A crackling blaze in a central firepit took a little of the chill from the air. Phillipe glanced from face to face surreptitiously as he entered the walled tavern yard. The patrons seemed oddly subdued; the range of expressions that he saw ran from mean to indifferent. A sullen barmaid moved silently among the tables. Just beyond the wall a blacksmith worked at a stable forge.

The patrons went on talking in desultory tones, not even glancing up as Phillipe moved past. No one showed the slightest interest in him, or even his borrowed clothes. At first he was only relieved; but as the moments passed, his ego began to prickle. Surely they couldn't get that many strangers in this town. He might be small, but he wasn't invisible. After all, he was Phillipe Gaston, who had escaped from the dungeons of Aquila and lived to tell about it.

Impulsively, he pulled out his heavy money purse and dropped it on a table in front of the barmaid. "A drink of your most expensive," he said in a loud voice. "And the same for anyone who'll join me in a toast!" This time the patrons did glance up at him in curiosity; but only for a moment, before they all turned back to their own conversations.

The barmaid returned, carrying a heavy earthenware mug. Phillipe looked critically at her as he took the drink from her hand. "Not much of a recommendation." He jerked his head at the drink. She shrugged and walked away without answering. Phillipe began to wonder uncomfortably whether the whole town was under some kind of spell.

"Let's hear your toast," a voice said suddenly, behind him.

Phillipe turned. An enormous, surly-looking man wearing a heavy cloak stood up, moving toward him.

"We drink to a special man, my friend," Phillipe said recklessly. "Someone who's been inside the dungeons of Aquila and lived to tell the tale." He raised his mug and took a long drink.

The stranger's mouth quirked in an unpleasant smile. "Then you drink to me, little man. My name is Fornac, and I've seen those dungeons."

Phillipe looked the other man's thick-necked, heavily muscled body up and down, nonplussed, and grinned at what he assumed was a joke. "A blacksmith, perhaps. A woodsman, or even a stonecutter. But a prisoner from Aquila?"

"I didn't say I was a prisoner." Fornac reached up to his throat, unhooking his cloak. He threw it off. Beneath it he wore the blood-red uniform of the Bishop's Guard.

Phillipe froze, as other men began to rise from the tables, removing their cloaks. The regular patrons sat numbly, their faces taut with fear. Their strange behavior suddenly made perfect sense to him, now that it was too late. More than a dozen guardsmen had surrounded him, silently drawing their swords. A small curse escaped him as he watched Jehan rise from a dice game near the fire with the Captain of the Guard at his side.

"If you'd stuck to the woods you might have stood a chance, Gaston," Marquet said.

"You're right," Phillipe said miserably. He stared at the half-eaten meal on a nearby table with a kind of desperate longing, before he cleared his throat. "That is ... actually I was trying to find you, Captain." Marquet stared blankly at him; he rushed on, stumbling over the words. "One of your men was cruelly murdered not far from here. But you're in luck. I'm willing to exchange the name of his killer for a pardon from you." Phillipe realized, hopelessly, that this time it even sounded unbelievable to him.

Marquet glanced at Fornac. "Kill him," he said.

Fornac lunged forward with his sword out. Phillipe threw his drink into the guard's eyes and dove under the nearest table, slipping away through the villagers' legs like quicksilver.

A group of guards rushed for the heavy table and turned it over, dumping food, plates, and pitchers heedlessly over the patrons and onto the ground. There was no one beneath it.

"There he is!" Fornac shouted. Phillipe darted

out from behind a man sitting at the next table—
straight into the waiting arms of another guard.

"Got him!"

Phillipe squirmed wildly until he freed an
arm. Planting a well-aimed elbow in the guard's
face, he broke away and disappeared back under the tables.

The guards leaped after him, searching every
corner, upending tables and hurling chairs aside
in heedless anger, throwing the courtyard into
pandemonium. Patrons screamed and ran; the
guards forced them back as they tried to flee
the yard. But Phillipe the Mouse seemed to
have disappeared into thin air.

A sudden silence fell, as Marquet glared with
deadly intent from one frightened face to another. Then the silence was broken by a shriek
from the edge of the courtyard. Phillipe crawled
out from behind the voluminous woolen skirts
of an immensely fat and immensely indignant
middle-aged woman.

"Purely unintentional, madam," he gasped
in apology. Looking frantically right and left,
he faced the gauntlet of guards that waited
between him and the gateway. This time there
would be no escape. He was a dead man even
if he surrendered. He pulled his dagger defiantly,
unable to think of anything else to do, and
leaped back into the crowd, struggling toward
the entrance of the yard and freedom.

Watching Phillipe's progress, Marquet pushed
through the patrons on a course of interception,

as inevitable as night following day. A guard
caught Phillipe's arm just as Marquet arrived
behind him, wrenching him around. Phillipe's
free dagger hand swung in a wide arc through
the air—raking Marquet's cheek with the tip of
the blade.

Marquet stopped dead in front of his prisoner,
his face frozen in a mask of rage. Blood trickled
down his jaw from the jagged scratch. His hand
rose slowly, touched the blood, confirming the
reality of the wound.

Phillipe sagged in the guard's grasp, equally
aghast as he realized what he had done, and
what it was going to mean for him. "I'm . . . so
terribly sorry. . . ." The words tumbled mind-
lessly out of his mouth.

Marquet gestured to his men. Two of them
jerked Phillipe back against a roof pole, pinning him there; a third raised his broadsword
over their helpless prisoner. Marquet grinned,
lifting his hand.

Phillipe turned his face away, his eyes
squeezed shut. "May God help me!" he cried.

Out of nowhere, a crossbow bolt struck the
guardsman in the arm; he dropped his sword
with a shout of pain.

"Marquet!"

Marquet froze, as he recognized the voice
that called his name. He turned slowly, and his
men turned with him, to see the figure of
Navarre standing like a deadly shadow at the
courtyard entrance. His broadsword swung ready

in his right hand, and a loaded crossbow rested in the crook of his left arm.

Marquet's eyes widened as they confirmed what his ears had told him. Phillipe slid to the ground as the guardsmen let him go, too stunned even to move. The yard around him was deathly still.

"One of my men told me you were back," Marquet snarled, his eyes never leaving Navarre. "I wanted to cut out his tongue for lying, because I knew you weren't that stupid." He glanced at Jehan. "Forgive me, Jehan. You are restored to your former rank."

Navarre shifted slightly, gestured to Phillipe. "You. Get out of here."

"Yes, sir," Phillipe mumbled. "Thank you, sir. . . ." Pulling himself together, he stumbled to his feet and ran out of the courtyard.

Chapter Five

Navarre stood like an obsidian statue, blocking the courtyard entrance while the young thief ran past him into the street. Then he called out abruptly, "Marquet. Look at me." Marquet's eyes came back to him from watching the boy flee. They burned with deadly hatred—almost as deadly as his own hatred for Marquet. He gazed at the man who had stolen the life that was his by right, and helped to destroy everything that had ever had any meaning for him: Marquet, the sadistic, craven bully; the Bishop's willing henchman. "I promised God my face would be the last thing you ever saw."

But as he lifted his crossbow a guard rose from behind an overturned table, aiming his own weapon, and fired. Navarre caught the

motion from the corner of his eye, turned
and fired almost simultaneously. The guard's
arrow whizzed past him, inches from his face.
His own bolt did not miss. The man crashed
down behind the table with a cry.

Navarre spun back, searching for Marquet—
and found himself face to face with another
guard, a man he recognized. The guard raised
his sword; lowered it again as their eyes met,
his face filling with uncertainty and deep regret.
"Captain," he murmured to Navarre, "I . . ."

Marquet's heavy boot slammed savagely into
the guard's back, shoving him forward, impal-
ing him on his former commander's sword.
Marquet leaped aside, roaring at his men to
attack. To a man they obeyed.

Navarre fought with the furious intensity of
someone obsessed, as if this fight were all that
he had been living for. But even with his almost inhuman reflexes, he was only one man,
armed with one sword, against more than a
dozen. The guards pressed him hard on every
side, cutting off any retreat, driving him back
through the mass of fleeing patrons toward the
fire. He ran another man through—not one that
he knew, this time. Sparks flew from the clash
of steel on steel; his sword arm ached from the
shock of a hundred blows. But his skill never
faltered. He gave ground slowly, and one by
one there were fewer attackers to surround him.

But Marquet was a man equally obsessed.
His nemesis had returned, and set free the pris-

oner whose life was worth more to the Bishop than his own. Navarre had come back, to reclaim all that was rightfully his; and Marquet's hatred doubled with his secret fear. He elbowed his way through the panic-stricken crowd, as Navarre was forced back to the very edge of the firepit, barely clear of the flames.

Navarre looked up to see Marquet advancing, murder in his eyes. Navarre killed another man almost instinctively, shoved him at Marquet as he pulled his sword free. Continuing the arc of his motion, he swung his sword at Marquet's head. His sword glanced along the captain's helmet, slicing off the golden eagle wings, the insignia of his rank. Marquet's face contorted with fury as he realized that Navarre had done it intentionally.

Navarre smiled grimly. Reaching behind him, he jerked a blazing branch from the firepit and drove it at Marquet's face. Marquet leaped aside, lost his balance, and tumbled into the fire. Guards rushed to his aid, dragging him from the pit and beating out the flames on his cloak. Navarre seized his chance in the confusion and began to fight his way back toward the exit.

Outside in the street, Phillipe pushed himself away from the wall of the nearest building and forced his leaden feet to move, stumbling with shock and exhaustion. He looked back at the tavern, still hardly able to believe what had just happened, or that there were still no guards in sight. Turning the corner blindly, he blun-

dered into the tethered horses the guardsmen
had hidden in the stableyard beside the tavern.
He jerked to a stop, keeping his feet by an
effort of will; he was struck with the sudden
inspiration that one of these horses would probably improve his now shaky escape chances by
one hundred percent.

But he had never ridden a horse in his life.
Horses terrified him. The animals, so massive
beside even a large, heavy man, seemed to loom
over him like mountains. Under normal circumstances he would never even have considered
this insanity. But these were hardly normal
circumstances. He untied the reins of the nearest horse with fumbling hands. Grabbing hold
of the saddle, he tried to get his foot into the
stirrup. Sensing his nervousness, the horse flattened its ears and shied away from him.

"Nice horse," Phillipe soothed unconvinc-
ingly, "good horse. . . ."

The horse jerked back and bolted away down
the street.

Phillipe looked tensely toward the tavern.
The shouts and screams, the clash of metal,
told him that the fight was still going on. Navarre
was holding off the entire company of guards
single-handed. For a fleeting instant it occurred
to him that he should go back and help the
man who had just saved his life a second time.
Just as swiftly, he realized that the idea was
not only suicidal but completely absurd. He

pulled the reins of the next horse free and
jammed his foot into the stirrup.

He held on to the saddle, boosting himself
up, without seeing the dangling cinch strap.
The saddle slid off the horse's back and crashed
to the ground on top of him. Cursing with
frustration and humiliation, Phillipe ran to the
next horse.

Back in the yard, Navarre slashed another
man's sword arm, watched blood spurt and the
other's sword fly free. His own body smarted
with cuts, none of them serious. His reaction
time was slowing; but only two guards and a
few more feet separated him from the gateway.
He pressed his attack with fresh determination,
inching his way toward freedom. Marquet was
still alive; but he had accomplished the thing
he had come to do, the truly vital thing—he
had saved the young thief.

Navarre knocked a last guard aside with the
flaming brand and sprinted out of the courtyard.
Glancing down the street as a riderless horse
cantered by, he saw, with incredulous dismay,
that Phillipe Gaston was still in view. The boy
stood in a milling herd of horses, trying vainly
to catch one after another. He looked up as
Navarre burst into view, and his own face filled
with dismay. He turned and ran.

Swearing furiously under his breath, Navarre
ran to his stallion and vaulted into the saddle.
The hawk, waiting on his saddlebow, spread
its wings and soared up into the air. Pulling his

horse's head around, he galloped away down the street after the boy. Behind him, one of the guards blew a warning call on a horn. Navarre looked ahead, his mouth tightening, knowing what it meant. *That damned idiot*, he thought, watching the boy run straight into another trap.

The town wall loomed ahead of them. The high wooden gate at the end of the street was open, but the guardsman stationed there had heard the horn blast. As Navarre watched, he began to push the gate shut.

Navarre's stallion bore down on Phillipe. The boy looked back as he ran, his expression a jumble of panic and terror. "No! No! No!" he cried. Behind them Navarre heard more horses galloping in pursuit. He glanced over his shoulder, saw Fornac and another guard riding hard after him.

He looked forward again, just in time to see the heavy gate slam closed ahead. Leaning down from his saddle, he thrust out his arm and scooped Phillipe up. The thief's small, wiry body scarcely strained his arm. He flung Phillipe across the front of his saddle like a sack of meal and dug his spurs into the stallion's flanks. The black's heavy muscles bunched as he gathered himself and leaped into the air. The stallion cleared the gate as if he were winged and landed at a dead run on the other side. The guard waiting at the gate lunged at them as they flew past; Navarre smashed the man in the face with his fist.

Navarre looked back, steadying Phillipe's groaning body with his hand. Behind him their two pursuers cleared the gate with far less grace. He caught up the sling that hung from his saddle and thrust a stone into it. Whirling it over his head, he let the stone fly. It struck the rider beside Fornac in the head, knocking him from his horse. But the awkward burden of Phillipe slowed his own stallion, and Fornac was still closing fast.

Navarre glanced up into the sky. The hawk wheeled in the blue heavens high above him, its silhouette like a drawn crossbow. "Hoy!" he shouted.

The hawk screeched and plummeted down through the air, its talons flashing like knives as it dove toward Fornac. The guardsman flung up his arm with a bellow. He pitched from the saddle as his horse reared, sprawling heavily on the ground. Navarre rode on without looking back, as the hawk soared triumphantly over his head.

Standing in the muddy street before the tavern, Marquet squinted from beneath his singed brows as Navarre and the thief disappeared into the forest. His smoke-blackened face hardened into stone. He turned back to his remaining men, all of whom were nursing wounds of their own. None of them met his eyes.

The hawk circled lazily in the warm updrafts that rose with the mountain wall. The long, sensitive primary feathers of her wingtips and the broad fan of her tail flared, twisted, narrowed, as she manipulated them with the delicate precision of fingers on a hand. Far below her, the man in black rode slowly through the blazing colors of the autumn forest along a narrow ridgeline. Perched behind him on the stallion was the smaller figure of a second rider, whose drab peasant clothing blended well with the forest floor. The hawk studied the pair of riders for a long time with expressionless golden eyes. At last she shifted her wings, increasing their drag, and began to drift down and down, until she settled at last on Navarre's gauntleted wrist. She flared her wings once, gazing up at him. Navarre smiled faintly in acknowledgment.

Phillipe peered past Navarre's broad shoulder to look at the bird, grateful for any distraction that would take his mind off the ride. Now that his life was not in immediate danger of ending for the first time in days, he had found himself with unexpected time in which to reflect on his new situation. But unfortunately, all that he seemed to be able to think about was how much he still hated horses. He had slipped in and out of an exhausted doze all through the afternoon, waking with every sudden lurch over the uneven ground, while his empty stomach endured a previously unknown form of motion sickness. He decided that this year he would give up horses for Lent.

He studied the preening bird, admiring the

subtle shadings of brown and olive on its smooth feathered back, its soft, cinnamon-streaked breast and black-striped tail. He was impressed in spite of his circumstances by its beauty, and by its ferocious loyalty to its master. Navarre wore no jesses or straps to keep the hawk always at his command. It came and went as it pleased, always returning to his arm. "That is a truly remarkable bird, sir," Phillipe said, attempting conversation for the first time in hours. Navarre was a man of few words, and in his grim presence, Phillipe had obediently been the same. "I'd swear she flew at those men of her own free will!"

Navarre glanced back at him. "We've traveled together awhile. I suppose she feels a certain ..." he hesitated, "... loyalty to me." The hawk trained a beady eye on Phillipe and hissed defiantly, flaring her speckled wings. Suddenly he felt that the bird was in no way this man's property ... that they traveled as equals. And that he was very definitely an unwelcome addition to their relationship, at least as far as the bird was concerned. But what about Navarre? The man who dressed like a mourner and fought like an angel of death plainly had some grudge against the Bishop's Guard; but that didn't change the fact that he had risked his own life twice to save the life of a total stranger they happened to be hunting. Once, it could have been a lucky coincidence;

but not twice. It was almost as if the man had
been following him. . . .

Phillipe cleared his throat. "If . . . you don't
mind, sir, perhaps you could explain a certain
loyalty which you seem to feel to me." This
time Navarre did not respond, or even look
back. Phillipe went on, pressing for an answer
that was suddenly important to him. "It's just
that you've saved my life twice and . . . I'm
nobody!" Realizing how that sounded, he added,
"Well, I'm somebody, of course. . . ."

Navarre rode in silence for another long
moment, thinking carefully. Thinking about the
truth, and about why he needed this remarkable mass of contradictions who clung to the
saddle behind him. Weighing what he had seen
of Phillipe Gaston's potential so far against the
possibility of telling him that truth. The words
rose up inside him—the sudden, terrible need
to share his burden with someone. . . . But not
this one. Not yet. He forced himself to remember that the boy was only a common thief, a
quick-tongued liar with no honor and probably
no future. He had seen enough of those to know
better than to trust one, even one with such
spirit.

He closed his mouth and thought for another
moment, remembering their first meeting. He
smiled to himself, out of Phillipe's view. "I
began thinking about what you said to me that
day on the bridge."

"Aha," Phillipe said, "I see." There was a moment of silence. "What did I say?"

"That I would be needing a good man to watch my flank."

He felt Phillipe straighten up behind him with sudden surprise and pride. "One does what one can," Phillipe murmured, in a fair imitation of modesty. After another moment he asked, nonchalantly, "Did you happen to notice that wicked gash across Captain Marquet's cheek?"

Navarre swiveled in his saddle, looking back in curiosity.

"He asked for it."

Navarre's eyes turned bleak, as he thought of how much more Marquet deserved. But seeing the boy's expression, he only nodded gravely, one warrior acknowledging another. He looked ahead again, to hide the smile that suddenly eased the tight, bitter line of his mouth.

Chapter Six

Fornac stood in the road outside the tavern with a hand pressed to his bandaged, aching head, overseeing the bloody job of loading the dead bodies of his fellow guardsmen onto an oxcart. Marquet had ridden back to Aquila to report to the Bishop. Jehan had taken the handful of men who were still able to ride and gone in pursuit of Navarre and Gaston. Fornac had been left in command of the cripples and the dead, which he realized was more of a rebuke than a compliment.

He shouted at the driver as the last body was dropped into the cart. The driver cracked his whip, and the cart lumbered away on its long journey to Aquila. Watching it go, he noticed an unexpected figure coming in his direction.

A fat, wheezing old man in the brown robes of a monk stopped to cross himself as the cart passed by. Then he continued along the muddy lane, precariously but resolutely. Fornac turned away and went in search of his horse, having come too close to needing last rites today for a conversation with a holy man.

The road was empty by the time Brother Imperius reached the spot where the guard had been standing. He stopped there, wiping his brow, gazing at the ruins of the tavern yard. For a moment guilt showed in his weary, blood-shot eyes. Shaking his head, he slipped his winesack from his shoulder and drank until it was empty. Then he started toward the tavern with the uncertain gait of a man who had drunk far too much already.

The innkeeper crouched in the courtyard, searching through the broken debris for anything salvageable. There was not much reward for his effort. He heard the sound of tankards clanking behind him and turned, shouting furiously, "Get away from that wine, you filthy bastards!" Too late he saw that the man who stood behind a charred table, pouring himself an enormous drink, was a monk. The innkeeper's face reddened. "Sorry, Father," he muttered.

The monk's shocked expression faded. "God has already forgiven you, my son," Imperius said kindly. He lifted the tankard and drained its contents before he said, "They tell me Etienne Navarre stopped by here not long ago."

"You might say that," the innkeeper answered sourly, thinking that word traveled fast.

"Did you happen to notice the direction he was headed in? It's crucial I find him."

"I'll tell you what I noticed, Father," the innkeeper said. "Swords, arrows, fire, and blood!" He flung a broken plate against the wall and watched it shatter.

Imperius nodded sadly and poured himself another drink. He downed the second tankard and wiped his mouth. "May God have mercy on you, and on those desperate enough to drink this wine." He put the tankard down and staggered out of the yard toward the road. The innkeeper shook his head.

Farther up in the hills, and later in the day, an isolated farm in a weedy forest clearing also received unexpected visitors. The middle-aged couple who eked out an existence there looked up from their endless round of labors as two men on one enormous black horse rode slowly out of the trees.

The woman, sweeping a futile cloud of dust out the front door with a ragged broom, stopped and stared, wiping her brow with greasy hands. Her eyes narrowed at the sight of the two men. The man in front, the one she could see clearly, looked dangerous ... but he didn't look poor. "Pitou! Pitou!" She ran across the yard, calling shrilly to her husband. Pitou studied the strangers from where he stood in the field beside the barn. His own eyes told him much the same story. The sickle he had been sharpening still hung in his grasp, and dark speculation filled his eyes. He ran a finger along the sickle's razor-sharp curve until a tiny line of blood formed on its tip. He put the finger into his mouth and sucked it thoughtfully.

Phillipe glanced around the farmyard as Navarre reined in the black. The tumbledown barn, the filthy yard, the cottage with its peeling walls and rotting thatch—this was not the sort of place he had anticipated spending the night in. But any human habitation was hard to come by this far up into the hills—and he knew that Navarre was just as much a hunted man as he was now. From Navarre's manner, and the weapons he carried, Phillipe suspected that he might have been a fugitive much longer. They had to take what they could get, for now. And besides, at this point he would gladly spend the night in hell itself just to get down off this horse.

Navarre made no comment, but Phillipe watched dubiously as their potential hosts for the night came forward to meet them. He had seen too many people like these—old before their time, embittered by hardship. The man's scrawny body was twisted from years of back-breaking labor on a starvation diet; the fat, blowsy woman in the grimy apron stared at him with eyes that were dull and dead, her heavy face a map of suffering. He had met far too many people like these ... and too many people who had tried to make one of them out of him. He pulled his ill-fitting stolen tunic back onto his shoulders self-consciously.

Navarre swung down out of the saddle. Phillipe slid down after him, barely keeping his feet as he landed. His body ached in so many places by now that the pains almost seemed to cancel each other out.

"Good day," Navarre said courteously. "I wish to impose on you for shelter tonight. For myself and"—he glanced at Phillipe—"my comrade-in-arms." Phillipe beamed and straightened his shoulders.

The man looked Navarre up and down cautiously, as if trying to decide how dangerous he was, or how much he might eat. "We have no food to share," he said. "But there's straw in the barn—for a price." His eyes never even touched Phillipe.

Stung, Phillipe pulled out his stolen money purse, jingling the coins patronizingly. "Bravely said, my dear fellow. But don't be frightened. We're not above compassion for those in misery—" He broke off. The gesture had not had the effect on the Pitous that he had intended. Instead of acknowledging that he was one with Navarre, and not with them, they merely stared as if mesmerized at the money pouch.

Navarre glanced sharply at him. He stepped

between Phillipe and the Pitous, cutting off their view. "Your dinner will be payment for our lodgings," he said. "Tonight you stuff yourself on rabbit!" He turned, signaling the hawk with an upraised arm. "Hoy!" The hawk exploded from the saddle, soaring up into the late-afternoon sunlight.

Within the hour they had not one, but two freshly killed rabbits for their dinner feast. Phillipe gathered wood and built a fire in the yard, at Navarre's orders, while the older man skinned the rabbits and spitted them on sticks. Navarre seemed uneasy about entering the Pitous' house, preferring to eat his meal out of doors. Phillipe was completely in agreement, all too familiar with the vermin and the stench they would probably find inside.

The Pitous joined them as the smell of roast rabbit filled the air. Phillipe had barely been able to control himself until the rabbits had finished cooking; the scent of freshly roasted meat made him dizzy with hunger. But the Pitous elbowed him aside, getting to the meat first; they ate ravenously and loudly, like wild animals. Watching them, he had forced himself to swallow his own meal with at least a semblance of calm and indifference. It was easier than he expected; his empty stomach had shrunken to the point where it held far less than he remembered.

Navarre ate desultorily, though he had not eaten at all during the afternoon, even after his battle at the tavern. The hawk sat perched on the peak of the barn above him. She screeched once, flaring her wings restlessly, and looked away toward the setting sun. Navarre raised his head at her cry, looked off toward the horizon as if he were following her gaze. He tossed a bone into the fire and rose slowly to his feet.

Phillipe glanced up at him. As he looked up, Pitou's bony hand snatched a half-eaten piece of meat from his plate. Phillipe looked back as the motion caught his eye. He shrugged with casual arrogance. "We eat like this every night." The knowledge that he would eat like this every night from now on made the lie more convincing.

He looked back at Navarre, who was still standing. Navarre's face, ruddy with sunset and fireglow, was the stark face of a man awaiting execution. A profound sadness welled behind his eyes. He walked silently past the fire and away, his tall, dark figure silhouetted against the bloody rays of the sun.

Phillipe stared after Navarre with curiosity that was half concern. Watching Navarre, he missed the speculative glance that Pitou gave to his own puzzled face. Pitou looked away at Navarre, and then at his wife, with a barely perceptible nod; her face tensed.

Navarre strode out past the ramshackle barn to where the black stallion grazed patiently among the weeds. He began to rummage in his

saddlebags, heedless of the others or what they
might think. His hands found the fluid softness
of cloth and the cold curve of burnished metal
with the ease of long familiarity. He drew out a
woman's gown of periwinkle-blue silk, and
the golden-winged helmet he had worn once in
his rightful place as the Captain of the Guard.
He stared at them for a long moment, lost in
memory, before he looked up again at the setting sun. "One day . . ." He repeated the vow
that he had made to himself—and to her—before
so many sunsets, that gave him the strength to
face the night ahead.

Phillipe rose from his place at the fire, aban-
doning the rabbit remains to the Pitous, and
followed Navarre quietly across the yard. He
got to within an arm's length of Navarre's back;
the other man did not even hear him. Phillipe
halted uncertainly, peering past Navarre's shoulder. He blinked in surprise as he saw a woman's
fine silk dress neatly packed among the supplies.
Navarre's hands pushed past it, searching for
something hidden deeper in the bag. He pulled
out a worn piece of parchment and unfolded it
carefully. The writing had grown so faint that
Phillipe could make out nothing but a single
capital letter I. Navarre's hands trembled.

"Sir?" Phillipe whispered.

Navarre spun around with the speed of a
striking snake. Phillipe saw tears shining in his
eyes, in the split second before those eyes filled
with furious rage.

Phillipe fell back a step, his heart constricting with the same terror he had known when he first saw Navarre. He opened his mouth, but for a moment nothing at all would come out. "If . . . there's nothing else I can do," he managed, "I think I'll turn in."

Slowly Navarre's face changed. The storm passed through his eyes, and was gone as suddenly as it had come. He ran a hand through his close-cropped, sandy hair. "There's a stall in the barn," he said brusquely. "Before you gather more firewood, see to my horse."

Phillipe swallowed a hard lump of unexpected irritation, nodded as agreeably as he could. He reached out for the black's reins with an uncertain hand, trying his best to imagine an ancient, docile cart horse. "C'mon, old girl, let's . . ."

The horse reared with an angry snort and shied violently away, jerking the reins from his hand. It fixed Phillipe with a furious stare, for all the world as though he had insulted it.

Phillipe smiled nervously. "Spirited little lady, isn't she? Ah . . . what's her name?" he asked, hoping that if he could get on more personal terms with the creature things would go better.

"Her name is Goliath," Navarre said.

Phillipe flushed. "Pretty name," he said, refusing to back down.

Navarre took the stallion's reins and handed them to Phillipe. "Go with him," he told the horse.

Phillipe was almost disappointed when the horse did not nod. He led the stallion away gingerly, talking all the while in what he hoped was a forthright manner. "Listen, Goliath. Before we get to know each other better, I feel I should tell you a story about this tiny fellow called David. . . ."

Navarre watched Phillipe and the stallion disappear into the creaking barn. A grin pulled his reluctant mouth up. Somehow the boy kept slipping past his guard, making him smile in spite of himself. He turned away, saw a patch of sunflowers still blooming among the weeds outside the barn door. He crossed slowly to them, looked down at their bright orange faces washed by the glow of sunset. He studied them wistfully, leaned down to pluck the largest one. He twirled it gently between his fingers, gazing out into the dusk, his thoughts far away from his present place and time.

The Pitous watched him from their place by the fire, glanced at each other with a knowing smile. Pitou slashed another piece of meat from the rabbit with a savage motion, and they went on eating noisily.

By the time Phillipe had finished his clumsy attempts at bedding down Goliath, darkness had completely fallen. Navarre was nowhere in sight, and even the Pitous had disappeared into their hovel for the night. Phillipe looked back at the barn with longing; the musty hay inside suddenly seemed softer than a down-filled mattress. Everyone on earth must be asleep now, except him. . . .

Navarre was not asleep, however; and Phillipe had the feeling that even if he were here to plead with, it wouldn't make any difference. The man was completely pitiless, with no compassion at all for the ordeal he had been through these past few days. Phillipe rubbed his burning eyes and trudged wearily into the forest at the edge of the clearing. He began to collect dead branches and brush, grateful that at least he had bright moonlight to work by.

After what seemed like an eternity, he started back through the trees toward the farm with an awkward armload of branches. The wood caught in his clothing and on every imaginable obstacle, and every time he bent down to pick up a branch that he had dropped, two more fell out of his arms. He staggered on toward the barn, muttering angrily. " 'Comrade in arms.' 'Slave' is more like it." He deepened his voice in a mocking imitation of Navarre, " 'See to the fire, feed the animals, gather the wood. . . .' " Navarre was no better than the rest. He looked up imploringly. "Look at me, Lord. I was better off in the dungeons of Aquila. My cellmate was insane and a murderer, but at least he *respected me!*"

He broke off, suddenly remembering that he didn't know where Navarre was. Navarre might even be watching him now, as he had apparently watched him for the last two days. Phillipe glanced back over his shoulder uneasily. "He's a strange one, Navarre," he muttered, more to himself than to God. He was no longer certain that Navarre was quite sane. "And he wants something from me. I can see it behind his eyes." Now that he had the time to think about it, he was sure that Navarre had not told him the real truth. He had been a fool to believe even for a moment that someone like Navarre actually considered him a fellow warrior. He was nothing to Navarre but a thing to be used.

He stopped moving all at once, clenching his teeth, as the unbearable tension of the past week suddenly overwhelmed him. He threw down the wood in angry refusal. "Whatever it is, I'm not going to do it!" he said loudly. "And besides, being in the service of a moving target is not my idea of steady employment!" Nothing answered him but the wind. "I'm still a young man, you know!" he shouted back toward the barn. "I've got *prospects!*"

A twig snapped loudly somewhere in the darkness nearby. Phillipe froze, listening. He heard more rustling in the bushes, suddenly chilled by the thought that something—or someone—actually was watching him. "Hello?" he called, wanting and not wanting to hear an answer.

Silence. Another tiny *snap*. Silence again. Phillipe's eyes narrowed as he looked around him, seeing nothing but impenetrable darkness between the trees. He cursed himself for not bringing his dagger, or even a light. All he had to defend himself with was his wits. "Who do you think's out there?" he said loudly. "Pierre, you'd better draw your sword! Ah, Louis, you brought your crossbow! We'll *all* go back to the barn now."

He answered himself in muffled voices, "Right! . . . Yes . . . Okay." He turned, listening; heard the sounds behind him in the woods more clearly now as they moved his way like measured steps. Whatever or whoever was stalking him was not impressed. The back of his neck prickled. He backed up a few steps, turned around again, and began to walk quickly in the direction of the barn. The presence followed him, matching his pace. Struggling to stay calm, he began to jog. Whatever was behind him picked up speed, keeping perfect time.

Phillipe panicked and ran. He bolted blindly through the trees, swatted by branches and scratched by thorns. His pursuer crashed through the brush after him. At last he burst out of the woods into the clearing, pulled himself up short with a gasp of relief. He turned, looking back—

Moonlight gleamed on the razor-sharp blade of the sickle in Pitou's hand. The farmer's eyes shone maniacally as he brought it down in an arc toward Phillipe's head. Phillipe threw up his hands, crying out.

A ghastly snarl filled his ears as something huge and black sprang past him. Phillipe gaped in disbelief as an enormous wolf struck Pitou down, its fangs tearing at the farmer's throat. He stood for an endless moment staring, as Pitou struggled futilely in the vise of its jaws. Then he turned and ran to the barn. "Sir! ... Come quickly, sir! ... Wolf! ... Wolf!" He crashed through the entrance, flinging the barn doors wide. "Sir! You must come!" Navarre was nowhere in sight. Phillipe slid to a stop, spun around desperately. Navarre's longbow rested against the barn wall in a shaft of moonlight. Phillipe grabbed it up, snatched an arrow from the quiver, and ran to a wide crack between boards. He peered through, sweat trickling into his eyes. Outside the screaming had stopped, but the snarls continued as the wolf crouched over Pitou's body, finishing its grisly work. Phillipe wiped his forehead on his sleeve, and nocked the arrow in the bowstring. Taking aim at the wolf, he tried to draw the bow. His arms strained until they shook; the heavy arch of wood barely gave. He relaxed his grip, panting; realizing, exasperated, that the bow belonged to a man twice as strong as he was. He raised the bow again, throwing all the strength of his panic against the unyielding wood. Slowly, the bow began to arch.

A hand draped in black reached past him and flicked the arrow from the bowstring.

Phillipe spun around. "But sir! There's a ..." He broke off, struck dumb by the sight before him.

Navarre's black-and-crimson cloak shrouded the ethereal figure of a slender young woman. Beneath the folds of its hood her skin was as white as alabaster in the moonlight, her hair shone like silver; her luminous green eyes studied him with a strange fascination, as if she had not looked on another human face in a long time. He stared back at her, because he had never in his life seen a face as beautiful as hers. The beauty was not so much in the perfection of her features, he thought, as it was in the radiant spirit that shone in her eyes. In her hand she held the golden blossom of a sunflower, twirling it between her long, delicate fingers as she smiled back at him in gentle bemusement. "I know," she said, and for a moment Phillipe couldn't even remember what it was she knew.

The wolf howled in the yard outside, a wail of bitter desolation. The woman's eyes flickered toward the sound, her face filling with a strange emotion.

"Who. . . ?" Phillipe whispered, trembling.

The woman only turned away, passing him silently as she drifted toward the barn's entrance.

Phillipe flung up a hand. "Don't go out there! There's a wolf! The biggest one you ever saw! And a dead man!" She seemed not even to hear him. "Miss? My lady? Please!" Phillipe cried helplessly, as she disappared through the doorway.

Phillipe shut his eyes, bowing his head as he

waited, breathless with dread, for a scream which did not come. Slowly he opened his eyes again, blinking toward the empty doorway. He slumped against the barn wall, his damp hands tightening on the smooth wood of Navarre's bow. "Maybe I'm dreaming," he murmured. "But my eyes are open. Which means that maybe I'm awake and just dreaming I'm asleep. Or more likely—maybe I'm asleep and dreaming I'm awake and wondering if I'm dreaming. . . ."

The shining woman's voice floated softly through the doorway. "You are dreaming."

Phillipe slapped himself hard in the face and leaped to his feet. He ran across the barn, flung himself up the rickety ladder into the loft. Scrambling through the hay to the star-filled rectangle of the loft opening, he lay flat on his stomach, looking out and down.

Below, in the silver wash of moonlight, he saw the woman move slowly out into the yard. The cloak billowed behind her in the breeze that stirred the leaves. Pitou's body lay still at the far edge of the clearing, by a lean-to woven out of sticks and branches. The wolf watched from a distance as the woman went to the body and stood gazing down at it. Phillipe could not tell what her expression was. She leaned over and covered the dead man with his cloak. Then she turned to look at the wolf, her eyes filled with anger and grief that Phillipe somehow knew had nothing to do with Pitou, or what the wolf had done to him.

The wolf was a huge one; Phillipe guessed that it must weigh over a hundred pounds. Its thick, coal-black fur was limned with silver, like the woman's hooded figure. It began to drift in her direction as she stood waiting serenely in the moonlight. Phillipe clenched his fist, bit down on it.

The wolf circled the woman warily, drawing closer, edging away, its fur ruffling, its wild amber eyes never seeming to leave her face. The woman smiled, the way she might smile at a beloved friend. She put out her hand, beckoning the animal to her. The wolf approached cautiously, sniffing. Its dark-stained jaws opened; Phillipe stopped breathing.

The wolf took the woman's arm in its jaws. But the glistening fangs drew no blood. The jaws closed ever so slightly, in what was almost a caress, then let her go. She knelt down, her arm gently circling the animal's neck. The wolf shuddered under her touch, then hung its head in docile acceptance of her affection.

Phillipe pushed himself away from the opening, unable to bear what he saw any longer. He sat in the straw, trembling again, harder than before. Looking up into the darkness, he whispered, "I have not seen what I have seen, Lord. And I do not believe what I believe." He had heard endless stories of magic and witchcraft, but he had never seen it happen with his own

eyes. Fear of the known was terrible enough—
"These are magical, unexplainable matters, and
I beg You not to make me part of them. . . ." But
even as he prayed for deliverance, he knew
that it was already far too late.

Chapter Seven

Marquet had ridden through the day and the night without rest, running three horses into the ground, barely stopping long enough to get a fresh mount at the guard posts along the road. At last, early in the morning of the new day, he saw the walls and towers of Aquila rise ahead of him on the plain, still miles away. He lashed his sweating horse with his quirt and galloped on.

Navarre was back—news more important than even Phillipe Gaston's neck or his own. Marquet rode grimly toward the city gates, clattered across the bridge and into Aquila at last, nearly riding down the guardsmen on duty. He galloped on through the streets without stopping, entered the sunken passageway that gave private access to Aquila Castle. Navarre was back, looking for vengeance—and the only man who had more to fear from Navarre than Marquet himself was the Bishop of Aquila.

Back in the hills, Phillipe and Navarre rode together through the new morning at a considerably slower pace. Phillipe watched silently as the hawk fluttered up through the trees, gaining speed as she soared into the open air. Ever since dawn, when Navarre's gauntleted hand had roused him, Phillipe had been trying to find the courage to tell the other man what he had seen in the night. A part of his mind wanted simply to believe it had never happened, while another part flinched from the thought of Navarre's acid scorn when he tried to describe it to him. But the part of his mind that knew what it knew desperately wanted some affirmation or denial.

Navarre reined in the stallion unexpectedly as they rode into a small, peaceful meadow. He dismounted. "We'll stop now. I need sleep."

Looking down at him, Phillipe saw the deep lines of exhaustion on Navarre's drawn face. Navarre walked away, dropped heavily to the ground beneath the shelter of a tree. Phillipe realized that Navarre must not have slept at all last night. He had never heard Navarre come back into the barn, through all the long hours when he had sat rigidly awake in the hayloft, staring into the darkness, listening to every eerie creak of the ancient boards . . . counting the seconds until morning. Then, somewhere just before dawn, his beaten body had surrendered to its needs, and he had fallen asleep so deeply that Navarre had had to shake him awake.

Phillipe still had no idea where Navarre had gone all night, or what he had been doing. But he was sure Navarre's disappearance and everything else were somehow related. He was even more certain now that Navarre was mad, if not possessed; and after all he had witnessed in the moonlight, he had no intention of asking him any embarrassing questions. But now he suddenly saw the opening for his own uncomfortable subject. He slid down from Goliath's back and crossed the meadow to Navarre's side. "I could do with a bit more sleep myself, sir. After last night's goings-on."

Navarre settled himself more comfortably among the fallen leaves, eyes shut, totally disinterested.

Phillipe hesitated. "That wolf could have killed me, but he tore out the farmer's throat, and left me alone." The thought struck him that it was almost as if the wolf had intentionally saved his life. In the morning there had been no sign of Pitou's body; but the blood-stained ground at the edge of the clearing bore mute witness that Pitou's death, at least, had been a reality.

Navarre yawned, his eyes still closed. This morning he had frowned, his face darkening

with an unreadable emotion, when Phillipe had
pointed out the proof of his narrow escape. But
then Navarre had simply turned on his heel,
striding wordlessly back into the barn to saddle his horse. The fact that they did not even
stop to cook breakfast but ate dried meat and
journeycake in the saddle as they rode was all
that told Phillipe the incident had even registered with Navarre. Disappointment and his
own reluctance had kept him silent the rest of
the morning . . . until now. "There was more,"
he said. No reaction. He took a deep breath.
"There was . . . a lady. Like fine porcelain, with
glowing jade eyes. A heavenly apparition from
some faraway land." The land of his dreams.
As he remembered her face again, his words
overflowed, "And her voice! The dulcet tones
of an angel—!"

Navarre's eyes popped open. "She spoke?"
he said.

Phillipe nodded eagerly. "I asked her if I was
dreaming. She said I was. Then, and this sounds
impossible to believe . . ."

Navarre shut his eyes again and rolled over,
turning his back.

Phillipe glared down at him. "I'm not insane,"
he said, his voice rising. "You must believe me
when I tell you these things." His words tugged
at Navarre's shoulder.

Navarre looked up at him, smiling sympathetically. "I do believe; I believe very deeply . . .
in dreams."

Phillipe's face fell. "I see." He began to turn away, defeated.

"This lady of your dreams. Did she have a name?" Navarre asked.

Phillipe turned back. "Not that she mentioned. Why?"

The smile was still on Navarre's face. "Since I'm about to fall asleep myself, I thought I might conjure her up for *my* dreams. I've . . . waited a long time to see such a lady as you describe."

Phillipe stared at him, more curious and more nonplussed than ever. He glanced away again as the hawk swooped down, landing on Navarre's saddle, as if she had been summoned by some unheard call.

"Now get some sleep," Navarre ordered. "The bird will alert us if someone comes."

"Heellp! Heellp!" The scream of a parading peacock echoed through the ornamental gardens of Aquila Castle like the cries of a terrified child. Marquet entered the courtyard like the Grim Reaper, sending the bird scuttling ignominiously aside. Friars and clerics glanced up from their muted conversations as Marquet strode past, oblivious to the beauty of this oasis of luxury in Aquila's desert of poverty.

At the far side of the courtyard Marquet spotted the Bishop's bodyguard and secretary; he angled past a sparkling, tile-walled fountain and headed in their direction. The Bishop sat beneath a mulberry tree, in intimate conversation with a striking young woman whose white, feather-decked gown mimicked the peacock's spreading plumage. The Bishop dropped a tidbit from the elaborate table of delicacies beside them into the woman's open mouth, like a man feeding a bird. Her laughter echoed through the garden. Behind them a young nun played a gentle tune on a lute; she broke off her song as Marquet approached their table without slowing down. The other clerics turned to stare with distaste at the sweat-soaked beast destroying the serenity of His Grace's garden.

The Bishop looked up from his conversation to see his Captain of the Guard materialize incongruously before him. His face grew rigid with displeasure as he held out his hand. Marquet bent to kiss his emerald ring, and a bead of grimy sweat dripped onto the Bishop's perfect white robes.

Marquet grimaced. "My apologies, Your Grace."

The Bishop gazed coldly at him. "Have you found the criminal Gaston?"

"He . . . is not in my custody at this time," Marquet mumbled.

The Bishop's frown deepened. "And yet you impose yourself upon this garden, unshaved, unwashed . . ."

"Navarre has returned," Marquet said bluntly.

The Bishop stiffened, feeling as though lightning had touched him. He glanced at his mistress, his face tightly composed. He nodded politely to her, excusing himself, and rose to his feet. "Walk with me," he said to Marquet.

He led Marquet along tile-edged walkways toward an unoccupied corner of the courtyard. Marquet outlined the encounter at the inn curtly, not meeting his stare. "The criminal Gaston travels with him. My men are combing the woods."

Together. They are together. The Bishop looked away with hooded eyes. It was a bad omen. Navarre had risked his life to save Gaston. It could only mean that Navarre knew the thief had found a way out of the city; a weakness in Aquila's defenses. A way out was a way back in. For his own safety, he must make absolutely certain that they were both destroyed.

He glanced back at Marquet again. "And the hawk?"

"Your Grace?" Marquet asked, his face blank.

"There should be a hawk," the Bishop said, with a little too much insistence.

Marquet nodded, suddenly remembering. "There is. Trained to attack. It unhorsed Fornac."

The Bishop smiled thinly, unable to disguise his satisfaction. "Yes . . ." he whispered. "This hawk would have . . . spirit." He looked up again, and Marquet tensed at the abrupt change in his expression. "The hawk is not to be harmed, is that understood?" He held Marquet's gaze relentlessly, his voice falling away to a harsh whisper. "You see, the day she dies a new Captain of the Guard will preside at your funeral."

Marquet nodded mutely, understanding that much perfectly.

The Bishop smiled again, at the fear and the confusion in his captain's eyes. *Always keep them unsure.* He turned in the path and led Marquet slowly back toward the garden entrance. "We live in difficult times, Marquet," he said conversationally. "This famine has prevented the people from paying their proper tribute to the Church." He gestured at the palace rising above them. "I raise their taxes only to be told there's nothing left for me to tax. Imagine." He stopped abruptly, searching Marquet's face again with sudden, fanatical intensity. Marquet stood still, riveted by his gaze.

"Last night the Lord Almighty visited me in my sleep," the Bishop said softly. "He told me that Satan's messenger traveled among us. And that his name was Etienne Navarre."

Marquet stared at him, his brutal face transfixed. He dropped to his knees, kissing the Bishop's ring again.

"Go." The Bishop gestured toward the gate. "To break faith with me is to break faith with Him."

Marquet rose and hurried to the exit, a man on a holy mission of extermination.

The Bishop turned to his secretary, waiting a few paces behind him. "Get me Cezar," he said. He had to be completely sure.

Navarre started out of a deep sleep as a sound he recognized almost instinctively set off alarms in his subconscious. His eyes snapped open; his body, tensed for instant action, lay obediently still. It was late afternoon already. His searching eyes found the hawk perched above him on a tree limb, perfectly calm, her head cocked curiously as she watched something below.

The sound came again—the *whoosh* of a broadsword through the air. Navarre raised his head and smiled. Resting on his elbows, he watched the young thief swing his broadsword again, with a look of vicious triumph, hacking at invisible enemies. The boy needed both hands just to lift the sword, and he staggered with every swipe of the blade, its weight and momentum dragging his small body around. Navarre pushed up onto his knees.

Phillipe chopped another attacker in two as he battled his way through the treacherous ambush toward his helpless lady love. Any other man would have been hopelessly outnumbered, but he was the Black Knight, who fought with the strength and skill of ten. He raised his sword for another blow—

And was spun around, as a black-clad arm wrested the sword effortlessly from his grasp.

Navarre drove the sword into the earth between them and sat back in the rainbow of fallen leaves beneath the tree. "This sword has been in my family for five generations," he said quietly. "It has never known defeat in battle." His blue eyes met Phillipe's brown ones with faint reproach, but he smiled. His hand reached out and caressed the sword's hilt.

It was a thing of beauty, as Phillipe had noted with awe and admiration. Two large jewels were embedded in the lower crosspiece, and one more partway up the handle. "This jewel represents my family name. This one, our alliance with the Holy Church in Rome." He touched the two stones in the crosspiece briefly. "This stone," touching the third, "is from Jerusalem, where my father fought the Saracens." His hand stopped, his fingers exploring the empty setting at the sword's hilt. He looked up at Phillipe.

Phillipe paled, as something far too knowing and expectant filled Navarre's gaze. Was this what Navarre wanted a thief for—to fill that hole for him by stealing a jewel the size of a bird's egg? Phillipe cleared his throat. "Sir . . . you don't think that I . . ." His hands brushed his chest.

"No," Navarre said darkly. "This is mine to fill. Each generation is called upon to find its special mission."

Phillipe let his arms drop, relieved, and cautiously intrigued. Navarre was actually confiding in him, and if it wasn't because he wanted him to steal, then perhaps Navarre really respected him after all. "And what . . . is your mission?" he asked expectantly. He saw himself riding off with Navarre on a knightly quest for the treasures of a glorious lost kingdom. . . .

Navarre looked up at him. "To kill a man."

Phillipe's face went expressionless. Disappointed, he said, "Well. I pity the poor wretch," thinking that at least it was a feat Navarre would have no trouble whatsoever accomplishing. It would be interesting to watch. "Does this walking corpse have a name?"

Navarre climbed slowly to his feet. "His Grace, the Holy Bishop of Aquila."

Phillipe blinked. "I . . . see," he said weakly. From personal experience, he knew that Navarre's reasons for wanting the Bishop dead must be excellent ones. But he was equally sure that he did not even want to know what they were. For a moment he had forgotten that Navarre was mad. The last gossamer wisps of daydream cleared from his vision as he clapped his hands together. "Well! Then you have . . . much to do and I've already been enough of a burden to you. I hope our paths cross again someday." He took a step backward, with a wave of farewell.

Navarre hesitated as he watched Phillipe begin to back away. He willed the boy to meet his eyes. "Come with me to Aquila."

Phillipe shook his head. "Not for the life of my mother. Even if I knew who she was." He took another step, glancing toward the trees.

Navarre bit down on his impatience. This moment was going exactly as badly as he had imagined it would. "I need your help to get into the city. You're the only one who's ever escaped from there."

"Escaped?" Phillipe laughed once, sharply. "I fell down a hole and followed my nose!"

"Then follow it back again!" Navarre snapped. He started forward, cursing the twisted fate that forced him to depend on this miserable human flea for his salvation.

"You don't want me with you on a mission of honor, sir," Phillipe pleaded. "I'm just a cutpurse, a professional thief!"

Navarre grabbed him by the front of his tunic, nearly lifting him off his feet. The boy cringed away from his gaze, from the animal fury Navarre felt rising in himself. He took a deep breath, forcing his mind to stay rational. Slowly and painfully, he tried to explain: "For two years I've waited to hear the warning bells of Aquila. Two years without a roof over my head, avoiding the Bishop's patrols, biding my time, waiting for a sign from God that the moment of my destiny had come." He looked down into Phillipe's wide, glassy stare, into the bright, resourceful mind he knew was hiding from him behind those frightened eyes. He smiled, a quiet, merciless smile. "And here you are, boy." He let Phillipe go.

"Me?" Phillipe pulled himself together swiftly, pulling his tunic smooth. He looked Navarre stubbornly in the eye. "Sir, the truth is, I talk to the Lord all the time, and . . . no offense . . . but He never mentioned you." He lifted his chin.

Navarre jerked his sword out of the ground,

swinging it back and forth easily with one hand. He looked at Phillipe again. "Perhaps—you forgot to ask."

Phillipe swallowed visibly, watching the barbed, razor-sharp blade slice through the air. His dark eyes turned grave. "Sir," he said, "I'm common as dirt. With common fears and common hopes for myself. There are . . ." He fumbled, for once at a loss for words. "There are strange forces at work in your life, magical ones which surround you. They are far beyond my ability to understand, but . . ." His voice faded. "They frighten me."

Navarre said nothing.

Phillipe grimaced. "You've given me my life— but the truth is, I can never repay you. I have no honor, never will have." He shrugged.

Navarre stared at him, his face unyielding.

Phillipe went on steadily, "I don't think you'd kill me simply for being what I am." He took a deep breath, and shook his head. "But better that than to return to Aquila." His fists clenched.

Navarre was suddenly aware of how small and defenseless the boy looked, and was; of how he must appear to the boy—a bully twice his own weight, armed with a sword, dragging him into a private vendetta that was probably suicidal.

Phillipe turned his back and walked slowly toward the woods. Navarre watched him go, watching destiny slip from his hands, and his last hope disappear. Phillipe began to walk

faster. Suddenly Navarre raised his arm and
hurled the broadsword like a javelin.

The sword smashed into a tree inches from
Phillipe's head. Phillipe spun around, looking
back with his heart in his throat. He saw the
look on Navarre's face—frozen, deadly; the face
of a man utterly obsessed. And he knew that he
had been wrong. Phillipe glanced again at the
sword quivering in the tree. He smiled ingratiat-
ingly as he leaned down, picking up a dead
branch, never taking his eyes off of Navarre. "I
think I'll gather some wood for the fire. . . ."

The night was quiet around the deserted
campsight; the embers of the untended campfire pulsed redly, like dying suns. Goliath
snorted and stamped, cropping grass, tethered
at the clearing's edge with Navarre's sheathed
sword slung at his saddle.

A twig snapped in the dark woods beyond
the fire. Goliath looked up, pricking his ears.
Another twig snapped. The young woman who
had called the wolf to her the night before
stepped cautiously out of the darkness. She
wore a man's tunic and pants, and a short
dagger at her belt. Her fair hair, uncovered, was
cut short like a man's, or a mourner's. She
entered the boulder-studded clearing, glancing
left and right, nervous but expectant. The clearing was empty except for the stallion. She
sighed, resigned to another night of solitude.
Goliath nickered softly in recognition. She

dropped another branch on the fire and crossed to him; offered her open palm for him to snuffle and lip.

Her eyes moved to the sword hanging from the saddle. She froze, as something wedged beneath its hilt caught her eye. She moved along the stallion's shoulder to pluck a hawk feather from beneath the sword. Holding it up into the moonlight, she marveled at the subtle patterns of light and darkness along its length. Her fingers traced its fragile profile delicately; she stood spellbound, as if she were touching a part of some creature to which she felt an uncanny kinship. She smiled, a smile for no one but herself. Her mind filled with dim echoes of soaring flight as she let the feather drift to the ground.

Reaching out, she uncinched the stallion's saddle, pulled it down from his back with the ease of long familiarity, and set it under a tree. She untied the rope of Goliath's halter. Goliath gave a brief snort of protest as she led him away from his meal.

"Oh, shush," she murmured. She tossed the rope across his withers. Reaching up to catch handfuls of his heavy mane, she swung easily onto his back. She smiled, stroking his neck. "Now, just make sure you remember everything we've learned," she whispered. She tightened her legs, and he moved forward, trotting slowly around the campfire. And then he began to dance. Responding to the subtle shifts of

her weight, the pressure of her gripping legs,
her almost inaudible commands, the war-horse
moved through the complex and beautiful dres-
sage patterns she had taught him through endless nights like this one.

As they circled the clearing like one creature,
in perfect communion, she could almost believe that she was back in her home in Anjou, a
girl again. If she closed her eyes, she could be
that other self, riding endlessly along the bright,
sunlit valley of the Loire through the colors of
the day. . . .

"Psst."

Her eyes opened. She halted Goliath instinctively, her heart pounding, wondering if she
were going mad at last . . . not willing to believe that she had actually heard another human voice whispering in the night. She peered
into the darkness around her, seeing nothing.

"Psst! My lady! Up here!"

She looked up, blinked in astonishment. Hanging from a stout limb just above her head was
the sweet-faced boy she had seen last night,
trussed up like a prize catch of game. His hands
were bound behind him, and the single long
rope that held him suspended circled his throat;
he could not even struggle. He looked exceed-
ingly uncomfortable. But he smiled at her, trying
hard to seem nonchalant. "Remember me?"

"What are you doing up there?" she said
incredulously. She realized it was probably
not what she should have said; but she had

almost forgotten how to speak to another human being.

"What am I . . . ah, and well you might ask that, yes indeed. . . ." The boy looked away from her, plainly thinking fast. "The Bishop's guards! A dozen of them! We had a terrible fight!"

She raised an eyebrow skeptically. "Why didn't they kill you?"

"Why didn't they . . . ah, yes, I asked them that myself!" He nodded, and winced.

"And?" she prompted.

"And?" he said blankly.

"What did they say?"

"Why, that . . ." He glanced toward heaven. "Uh, they preferred to leave that honor to the Bishop!"

She looked down, to hide her smile. She recognized Navarre's handiwork: He must have tied the boy up, leaving him helpless and out of harm's reach. But she had no way of knowing what his motives were. And what was the boy doing here at all? She had thought he was only some peasant's son. But he spoke too well— and was too good a liar—to be a simple peasant boy. Had he been following Navarre? She looked back at him, uncertain.

"Please, my lady?" the boy said pathetically. "A giant owl examined me quite carefully not one minute ago."

She studied him thoughtfully, considering the possible alternatives. No . . . she could not spend all night with that poor wretch dangling from a tree over her head. He looked harmless enough. Suddenly the yearning for human company, the sound of a voice that was not her own, became unbearable. She drew her dagger. Doubt and then gratitude filled the boy's eyes as she reached up and freed his hands. Sliding from Goliath's back, she severed the rope that bound him to the tree. The boy wriggled loose and dropped to the ground beside her, shaking out his numbed hands.

A wolf howled, somewhere in the darkness. She looked away toward the sound, her heart squeezed with sudden grief. The wolf howled again, and she turned back to the boy reassuringly. "Listen. There's nothing to ..." She broke off.

The clearing was empty. The boy had disappeared.

She grimaced with dismay, clenching her fists. She had forgotten even more than she realized about how human beings behaved. . . . Navarre would be furious. Suddenly she ached to hear his voice, even raised in anger, even shouting at her—a longing as deep and as hopeless as her longing for the sun. She shook her head, turning back in resignation to face the forest; listening, waiting.

Chapter Eight

Phillipe stumbled wearily through the brightening dawn. He had walked all night, eager to put as much distance as possible between himself and the haunted clearing. His face stung with scratches, his clothes were full of leaves and dirt from falls in the darkness; but it was a small price to pay to be free of Navarre. He began to climb toward the sunlit crest of another long slope; stopped, sniffing the air with sudden interest. He smiled. Somewhere over the hill, someone was cooking breakfast. He licked his lips, and went on climbing.

Meanwhile, miles behind him, Navarre entered the campsite with the sunrise, his own face lined with fatigue. He strode directly to the tree where he had left Phillipe. One look at the empty limb, the empty ropes lying on the ground below it, told him everything. His mouth thinned. She had set the boy free. Of course she would. She hadn't realized . . . he should have left her a note, should have warned her somehow. He struck the tree trunk with his fist, furious at his own stupidity and help-lessness. He turned away from the sight of his failure, back toward the dying fire, trying to tell himself that the boy had been hopeless anyway. That he had not really lost anything— that he had never even had it to begin with. . . .

The stallion snorted, and he glanced up; he stopped, staring. The sight before him was so incongruous that he would have smiled at it on the way to the gallows. Goliath stood beneath the tree, just as Navarre had left him last night. Except that during the night someone had braided the stallion's heavy mane and curled it into ringlets. The sunflower he had picked at the farm and left for her was woven into the horse's forelock. He had never seen a horse look embarrassed—until now. He crossed the clearing to the stallion's side, still grinning, and shook his head. "Poor bastard," he mur-mured, his throat tight, "you're defenseless against her too, aren't you?"

Phillipe crouched at the top of the hill, peer-ing downslope. In the valley below he could vaguely make out figures moving, half hidden by the thick smoke of their fire. Their garbled speech reached him faintly. There seemed to be a lot of them. He half rose, hesitated, weighing caution against hunger.

A heavy hand closed on his shoulder, jerking him around.

Phillipe's mouth fell open, but he had nothing to say to the burly guard whose hands gripped him like a vise. The guard grinned broadly. "Join us!" he said. He pushed Phillipe over the brink of the hill.

Phillipe tumbled crazily down and down, head over heels through the rocks and brush, until he hit the bottom. Lying sprawled on his back, he struggled to raise his head as another set of uniformed legs loomed over him. He blinked his eyes clear and looked up at his captor.

"Well, well," Fornac said. "You're a long way from the sewers, little rat. This time the drinks are on me."

Phillipe rolled his eyes, let his head fall back with a small groan.

The other guards had come to stand around him in a group. Fornac grabbed him by his tunic and hauled him up to a sitting position. "Where's Navarre?"

"Navarre, Navarre . . ." Phillipe shook his mind loose frantically. Fornac lifted a mailed fist, held it clenched in front of his face. "Ah! Big man, black horse? He went south, along the road to Aquila." Phillipe waved a hand in what he hoped was the right direction.

One of the other guards smiled knowingly. "Then we ride north, right, sir?"

Phillipe sat up straighter. "It's not polite to assume someone's a liar when you've only just met him," he said, indignant.

Fornac studied him, frowned. "And yet you knew we would. . . ." he said slowly. "We ride *south*—toward Aquila!"

Phillipe cursed in silent frustration as his plan bit his own hand like a snake. Fornac's men dragged him to his feet and propelled him back toward the campsite. He knelt numbly while two guards shackled his hands together behind him. They boosted him up onto a tethered horse and tied his feet together beneath its belly. He sat watching the guardsmen break camp with frightening speed, eager for the hunt—eager for it to end with Navarre's death. Phillipe looked up into the sky, where heavy gray clouds were spreading across the sun. "I told the truth, Lord," he said morosely. "How can I learn any moral lessons if You keep confusing me like this?"

Fornac trotted up alongside him and took hold of his horse's reins. The guard troop rode out, heading south toward the Aquila road.

Navarre rode grimly down the Aquila road beneath a sky gray with lowering clouds. With or without the boy, he was going to the city. The Bishop of Aquila would die . . . or he would die, trying to reach the Bishop. It no longer mattered to him which; it only mattered that he was acting, now. He was through waiting for a sign which would never come. . . . And always, in the back of his mind, he knew that no matter how that final encounter ended, he had already lost.

A wind chill with the promise of winter moaned through the trees, swirling up clouds of dry leaves and dust. Navarre raised his arm, shielding his eyes. The hawk perched on his other arm, just below his elbow; she huddled against his side for protection and warmth.

A dead branch crashed down into the road beside him. The stallion shied; the hawk took to the air with a startled cry. Navarre steadied his horse with a soft word, looking ahead again. He saw nothing but open fields, some domed granaries and a distant flock of sheep. He urged the black forward into a canter, and rode on unknowingly into ambush.

Fornac and his men lay silently in the underbrush along the roadside, waiting and watching as Navarre rode into view. Phillipe lay on his stomach, surrounded by guards, a gag in his mouth and his hands manacled behind him. He lifted his head, his eyes filled with sick terror as he watched Navarre riding to his death. Navarre might be a madman; but watching that proud figure on his black stallion, Phillipe only knew that the man who had saved his own worthless life twice did not deserve to die like this. And deep in his mind was the aching knowledge that somehow this was all his fault.

Fornac nodded, and Phillipe heard the soft clicks of crossbows being loaded all around him. Phillipe chewed on his gag, grimacing and twisting his face, forcing it into the center of his mouth. Down the road he saw the stallion's ears prick forward, as if he sensed something ahead. Navarre slowed.

The gag slipped into Phillipe's mouth. He glanced from side to side, blinking hard as he looked at the armed men all around him. They would kill him instantly if he made the slightest sound to warn Navarre. But if he didn't, they would kill Navarre instead. . . . Phillipe shut his eyes, still not quite believing what he was about to do, and took a deep breath.

Suddenly, far above, a hawk screamed. The stallion reared up in the road as Phillipe opened his mouth to shout. The guard next to him looked around—and jammed a hand into his mouth.

Phillipe bit down hard. The guard bellowed.

"Fire!" Fornac shouted furiously.

A hail of arrows rained down on Navarre. Phillipe saw one strike him in the leg, saw blood splatter over his saddle. The hawk screeched in fury, diving down, as Navarre drew his sword and wheeled his horse around.

Phillipe, lying forgotten underfoot as the

guards reloaded, heard shouting and screams as Navarre fought off his attackers. Phillipe rolled over, pushing himself up onto his knees, searching for a chance to make his own escape. He saw Fornac look up at the swooping hawk, his face filled with rage. Twice now it had saved its master from him, and Fornac would not let the bird escape to save Navarre again. The guard raised his weapon, taking aim.

Gritting his teeth, Phillipe arched his body and jerked his manacled hands down his back. He squeezed his body through the loop of the chain and flung himself at Fornac from behind. Throwing the chain over Fornac's head, he pulled it tight. Fornac's hands flew up to his throat, grasping the chain. Phillipe threw all his weight against it; but all his weight was not enough. Fornac jerked it down, flipping Phillipe over his head. Fornac clubbed him aside with a heavy fist and leaned down to catch up the crossbow. Mounting his horse, he searched the battlefield and the sky.

The hawk was out of his sight now, swooping and diving to Navarre's aid, as the black stallion charged though the underbrush like a juggernaut. Navarre fought like a man possessed, driving the guards into retreat with the fury of his attack. But as they retreated, they suddenly left his back exposed, a perfect target in Fornac's line of fire. Fornac's eyes narrowed with satisfaction as he raised his crossbow for a shot that could not miss.

Phillipe struggled to his knees, seeing Fornac take aim. He caught up a rock and hurled it. It cracked against Fornac's helmet; Phillipe saw the arrow go wild, in the split second before pain exploded in his own head as another guard's crossbow smashed down on him.

He never heard the hawk's shrill scream, as the random shot pierced her breast. But Navarre heard it. He looked up, driving the retreating guards before him, to see her drop from the sky in a flurry of feathers, her wings beating helplessly. He cried out as if the shot had struck his own heart; the stallion reared as he jerked convulsively on the reins.

Beyond the guards, he saw Fornac sitting on his horse in the road, with his crossbow in his hands. Fornac grinned savagely. Navarre drove toward him with a bellow of fury, swinging his sword. Fornac raised his crossbow and fired again.

The shaft drove deep into Navarre's shoulder, knocking him from his saddle. His sword flew from his hand as he fell. He struck the ground hard; lay stunned for a long moment, gasping with pain. Lifting his head with an effort, he saw Fornac charge, raising his sword high.

Navarre pushed himself to his knees, weaponless and desperate. Looking down, he grasped the arrow shaft that protruded from his leg and yanked it out. He staggered to his feet with the arrow in his fist as Fornac's horse bore down on him. Dodging under Fornac's blade at the last instant, Navarre thrust the arrow up into his chest. The horse's momentum drove the shaft into Fornac's heart as the blow dragged him out of the saddle. Fornac was dead before he struck the ground.

The impact knocked Navarre away and down. He struggled to his feet again, covered with blood, his own and Fornac's. Searching around him, he found his sword and picked it up. The few remaining guardsmen who were still standing began to back away from him. Throwing down their weapons, they caught their mounts and rode back toward Aquila.

Oblivious, Navarre stumbled through the carnage along the road to the place where the hawk had fallen. Goliath trailed him like a great shadow. The hawk lay in the dust, with the arrow bristling from beneath her bloodsoaked wing; her fierce golden eyes were glazed with pain. He drove his sword into the ground and sank to his knees beside her, his hands knotting. Blood from his wounds stained the dirt where she lay, but he felt nothing of his own pain now. He lifted her with trembling hands. Gently he tried to clean her wound, to see how deep the hurt was. Too deep. He looked up, looking toward the west, where the sun floated like molten gold just above the crest of the distant hills. Tears of grief and rage welled in his eyes. He looked

down again at the hawk lying helplessly in his
hands. *God help me*, he prayed, for the first
time in years. *Help me*—

A shadow fell across him. Startled, he looked
up into the face of Phillipe Gaston. The young
thief stood staring down at him, pale and dazed.
Blood from a scalp wound trickled down his
neck. A chain swung from his shackled hands.
Phillipe's dark eyes filled with sorrow as they
gazed at the wounded bird. As they searched
his own again, Navarre saw something unreadable flash in their depths. For a moment he
thought the boy would turn and run away. But
Phillipe stayed rooted where he was, like a
dagger drawn to a lodestone.

Navarre had no idea what the boy was doing
here. He had no time to care. Leaning heavily
on his sword hilt, he pushed himself to his
feet, with the bird cradled in his hand. He held
the hawk out to Phillipe and said hoarsely,
"Take the bird. Find help."

"Me, sir?" Phillipe said in disbelief.

"I have no one but you."

Phillipe bit his lip. "Sir . . . the poor thing is
done for," he said softly.

Navarre ignored the words, keeping his feet
with an effort. "There's an abbey on top of a
mountain in those hills over there. In it you
will find a monk. Brother Imperius. Bring him
the hawk. Tell him she belongs to Charles of
Navarre. He will know what to do."

"Sir, I . . ." Phillipe raised his shackled hands.

"Kneel down." Navarre set the hawk down gently as he spoke, and pulled his sword from the earth. Phillipe obeyed, wincing as Navarre split the heavy chain between his wrists with one blow.

"Take my horse and go, boy. Now!"

Phillipe got to his feet and turned to Goliath. The stallion's ears flattened; he reared up, lashing out with his hooves. Phillipe leaped away. "But sir . . ." He looked back at Navarre. "You're the only one who can ride him, and . . ."

Navarre shouted a furious command at the black. The stallion calmed instantly, stood waiting with his ears pricked forward. Navarre's free hand caught Phillipe by the scruff of the neck. *"Do it, boy!"* He pushed him up into the saddle.

When Phillipe had settled himself, Navarre handed him the hawk, wrapped in a shirt from his saddlebag. Phillipe cradled the wounded bird gingerly in the crook of an arm. Navarre put the stallion's reins into his hand. "And know this," Navarre said, when the boy looked down at him again. "If you fail to reach that abbey, I will follow you the length of my days until I find you, and carve your wretched body into pieces fit for flies."

Phillipe's white face turned even paler. He nodded with absolute understanding, and started the horse away across the open field.

Navarre raised his hand to his shoulder, to

the crossbow bolt still jutting from it. He jerked it out. He shuddered with pain; but his eyes never left the figure growing smaller in the distance.

Chapter Nine

Phillipe looked back as he rode, saw Navarre standing like a monument carved from stone, his shadow thrown far across the battlefield by the setting sun. As Phillipe watched, the man of stone crumbled and fell. Phillipe looked ahead again toward the distant purple hills, his face set, urging Goliath on.

On the far side of the field he reached another road, which wound up into the hills Navarre had sent him toward. Goliath took the road willingly, seeming to know almost by instinct where they were headed. Phillipe held the bird as if it were made of glass.

Goliath moved as fluidly as water beneath him as they cantered up into the darkening hills, as if even the horse were trying to spare the hawk from pain. But the bird cried out, weakly, as they rode into the shadow of a massive stone cliff. Phillipe slowed the stallion, looking down at the hawk. "It's all right," he whispered, "I've got you." He looked up the face of the mountain; his breath caught.

Above him on the heights stood the ruins of a once-imposing abbey, caught in the rays of the setting sun. The stark lines of its crumbling, weather-eaten walls of stone were softened by a mass of ivy and vines. Its bell tower, still intact, watched over the valley below like a silent sentinel. This was what Navarre had sent him to find. He glanced down at the bird again. The shirt that wrapped the hawk was stained with red; the arrow standing out from beneath its wing looked fatally large against its small, fragile body. "There it is . . . see? The abbey!" He cupped a hand tenderly under the hawk's head, trying to reassure it. The bird's sharp, hooked beak snapped at his fingers.

Phillipe pulled his hand away, startled. "Well, *that's* gratitude. . . . All right then," he said, exasperated. "Let this Imperius fellow watch you die, I've got my own life to worry about!" He wondered irritably how even a madman could care so much for a thankless wild animal. "You're a witness," he told the stallion.

Goliath merely turned from the road, picking his way up the narrow trail that wound to the top of the peak.

Phillipe halted before the abbey's arching gate,

studied its heavy wooden door. He looked up
dubiously at the silent stone walls. "Hello! Hello
in there!" he called. Sparrows flitted in and
out of the ivy, the only sign of life he saw.
What if the monk had gone ...? "For pity's
sake—" he shouted, "hello!"

"Lower your voice out there, damn you!"
someone shouted back. "Do you think I'm deaf?"
A wild-haired old man in the brown-and-gray
robes of a monk peered owlishly from a parapet of the ruins. The monk's eyes roved at
random across the shadowed landscape, completely ignoring both horse and rider.

"Over here, Father!" Phillipe called. "Imperius—?"

The bloodshot eyes found him at last. The
monk gazed down on him blearily. "Curious,"
he mumbled, "that's my name too."

Phillipe realized with a twinge of dismay
that the man was drunk. "I was told to bring
you this bird. She's been wounded."

"Good shot!" Imperius cried heartily. "Bring
her in and we'll dine together."

"We can't eat this bird!" Phillipe shouted,
his anger rising.

"We can't?" Imperius shook his head. "Oh
my God, is it Lent already?"

Phillipe took a deep breath. "This is no ordinary hawk, Father," he said insistently. "She
belongs to Etienne Navarre."

Imperius blinked, stared down at them as if
his mind had abruptly cleared. "Mother of God,"

he whispered. "Bring her in! Quickly!" He turned away, pulling on the rope that unbarred the door below.

Phillipe dismounted, slowly and with difficulty, holding the hawk steady all the while. He turned, looking up at the stallion. "Wait here," he said.

The stallion whinnied suddenly, swung around, and galloped away down the hill.

"Tell him we got here!" Phillipe yelled. "Tell him I did my part!"

"Hurry up, you cretin!" Imperius called. "Get her up here!"

Phillipe turned back and hurried through the gate. Striding up through the inner courtyard, he saw a drawbridge lying open before the abbey's main entrance. Imperius stood on the bridge waiting impatiently for him.

As he started across the bridge, Imperius reached out, grabbing his arm. "*Careful*, you lummox!"

Phillipe looked down at the wide planks, seeing nothing abnormal, as Imperius pulled him over to the left side of the bridge.

"Walk on *this* side," Imperius insisted.

Phillipe shrugged and obeyed, following him into the abbey.

Imperius led him through dim, drafty corridors and empty cells, up steps worn into hollows by countless feet. Phillipe wondered fleetingly why anyone, even a monk, would choose to live in this dismal ruin all alone.

At last they reached a small room behind a massive, decaying wooden door. Yellow candlelight showed him a plain, solid table and chairs, books and writing implements, a cot covered by sheepskins—Imperius's own quarters, he guessed.

"Over there on the cot . . . easy . . ." Imperius directed.

Phillipe laid the bird on the bed with careful hands.

"Leave us alone," Imperius snapped.

"But . . ." Phillipe protested, remembering Navarre's threat with sudden vividness.

"Get out!"

Phillipe backed reluctantly toward the doorway and went out. The door slammed behind him, and he heard the sound of a lock clicking shut. He sat down on the stone floor of the hallway and pulled his dagger out of his boot. With its tip, he began to work at the locks on his manacles. Behind the door, he heard Imperius say softly, "Don't be frightened. Navarre was right—I can help you. . . . But we must wait."

The monk came out of the room again and glanced down at Phillipe.

"Is there anything I can do to help?" Phillipe asked.

"No, boy," the monk said brusquely. He shut the door and pointedly locked it from the outside before he hurried away down the hall. Phillipe went on working at his shackles.

Out in the monastery's weed-grown garden, Imperius worked by the light of a bonfire, gathering herbs. His mind was perfectly clear now; he moved with confidence among the plants, hurriedly clipping the perfect leaves, in the precise amounts he needed. As he worked he looked out again and again across the valley, looking westward, his face furrowing with concern. He watched the final flash of day send streaks of ruddy afterglow lancing up between the clouds. The sun had set. Placing the last of the herbs into a small stone mortar, he started back up the hill toward the abbey.

The second shackle dropped from Phillipe's wrist and clattered to the floor. He grinned with the satisfied pride of a skilled professional and shook out his hands. Climbing to his feet, he went back to the door of Imperius's cubicle. He fingered the heavy lock thoughtfully, then slipped his dagger point into its keyhole and probed. In a matter of seconds the ancient mechanism clicked open.

Phillipe opened the door quietly and entered the room. And stopped, staring in disbelief.

There was no longer a hawk on Imperius's cot. Instead, the fair woman who had haunted his nights lay there, covered with a fur robe, her arms spread in imitation of the hawk's wings. The crossbow bolt protruded from her shoulder.

Her eyes flickered open at the sound of his footsteps. She lifted her head to look at him, her eyes filled with agony. She tried to raise herself up. "Navarre! . . . Where is he? Is he . . ."

"He'll be fine, my lady!" Phillipe said hastily, holding up his hands. "There was a terrible battle with the Bishop's guards. Navarre fought like a lion. The hawk was . . ." He broke off, as his leaping thoughts suddenly caught up with the truth. He shook his head. "But . . . you know that, don't you?" he whispered.

The woman lay back. "Yes," she murmured, after a long moment.

Phillipe moved timidly to stand beside the cot. He looked down at her, astonished again at the heartbreaking beauty of her face. "Are you flesh?" he asked slowly. "Or are you spirit?"

Her fever-bright eyes fell away from him, staring at nothing. "I . . . am sorrow."

The door opened behind him. Imperius entered the room and stopped, aghast. "How did you . . . ?" He crossed the room, seizing Phillipe by the arm. "Get out, damn you! And *stay* out this time!" The monk shoved him out the door and slammed it behind him.

Phillipe stood still in the hall for a moment, then suddenly leaned back against the door's solid support, breathless and weak as the reaction to what he had just seen finally hit him. From inside the room he heard Imperius's voice again, like a prayer: "Holy Father—after all that's happened, You couldn't possibly have brought her here to die." Phillipe pushed himself away from the door and went hurriedly down the corridor, in desperate need of some fresh air.

He found his way out into the garden, stood studying the overgrown field and the makeshift outbuildings of the abbey yard in the bonfire's flickering light. A mule and some goats drowsed in a pen; chickens muttered and pecked after grubs. On a scarred weather-gray tabletop he saw a curious assortment of apples and oranges arranged in rings, as if the monk had been playing some sort of game. He wandered down the hill to the table and sat on a bench, his fingers rapping on the wood, studying the fruit arrangements with half his mind. . . . He supposed living alone in a ruin didn't provide many interesting pastimes. He glanced up again at the looming skeleton of stone high on the hill above him; searched out the abbey's single lighted room with restless eyes. A woman's anguished moan carried faintly to his ears. Phillipe turned back to the table. He picked up an apple and bit into it nervously.

Imperius stood at the table in his room, mashing the herbs with a pestle, his eyes never leaving the woman's face. Her own eyes were closed, and her arms shone with perspiration. She stirred and moaned again, drifting into a fevered dream. Imperius set down the pestle to lay a cool, wet cloth across her burning forehead. He returned to his work, held a candle beneath the mortar's bowl to warm the poultice he had made. Somewhere in the night beyond the abbey

walls a wolf howled mournfully; the woman's
body twitched beneath the coverings. Imperius
glanced up, set the steaming poultice on the
table. Turning back to the woman's side, he
packed the poultice around the wound as gently
as he could. The woman opened her eyes, gazing up at him as he reached for the arrow with
a reluctant hand.

In the garden, Phillipe took another bite from
the apple, blinking tensely as he stared out into
the darkness.

Imperius's hand closed over the arrow and
pulled it free. The woman screamed piercingly.

Phillipe jerked around, looking up; the apple
fell from his nerveless fingers.

In Aquila Castle, His Grace the Bishop lunged
upright in his canopied bed, wracked with terri-
fying pain. He stared wildly into the shaft of
blinding illumination that spotlighted him in
his private darkness; he looked down at himself in horror, and then in disbelief, as he found
no wound, no blood, no assassin's dagger. The
coils of nightmare fell away from him, and he
realized that it had been no more than a dream
. . . this time. He clutched the silken sheets and
embroidered comforters, gasping for breath.
Slowly his hands loosened; he wiped perspiration from his face as his eyes adjusted to the
light. He was in his own bed, safe within the
castle walls . . . and a frightened young acolyte
stood in the hallway outside his open door.

"I'm . . . sorry, Your Grace," the young monk said. "You insisted on being told when he arrived. . . ." He scurried away.

His place was taken by a vision out of hell. A huge, brutal figure filled the doorway, blocking the light. The lines of a scar marred his cheek above his scraggly black beard. His heavy fur cloak was of wolf pelts. A necklace of wolves' teeth circled his throat. He gazed at the Bishop with dark eyes far crueler than any animal's.

"Cezar," the Bishop said, and smiled.

Chapter Ten

The ruined abbey lay peacefully in the moon-light, as it had for centuries. The solitary black wolf limped to the line of a nearby ridge and stood gazing up at it from among the trees. Dried blood matted the thick ebony fur of the wolf's shoulder and hind leg. The bitter wind swirled around him as he settled down wearily, to begin a vigil whose reason he could not even comprehend. He lifted his head and howled his anguish at the waning moon.

Safe within the abbey's walls, Phillipe sat on a crumbling terrace step beside the bonfire, watching as Imperius poured a huge tumbler of wine with unsteady hands. The old monk glanced up at the darkness apprehensively as the wolf howled. Phillipe studied him through the dancing flames, suddenly very sure that the monk was not simply afraid of wolves. "It's him, isn't it?" he asked softly. *Navarre*. The monk didn't answer. "The wolf," he said again. "Somehow . . . it's him." Knowing that, the sound of howling no longer frightened him.

Imperius filled a second tumbler with wine, not even bothering to look at him. "Here. Get drunk. You'll forget."

Phillipe shook his head, leaning back against the stone step behind him. "An hour ago you were drunk. And you remembered."

Imperius looked up at him. Phillipe's eyes held the monk's insistently. He had told Imperius his own part in this strange dance of fate, more or less completely. And by bringing the hawk here, he had earned the right to know the greater pattern. He waited, his stare unyielding. Imperius slumped where he stood, defeated. Picking up his own drink, he crossed to the fire, sat down with a sigh of resignation. Phillipe pulled his feet up onto the wall, waiting.

The old monk glanced toward the lighted window in the abbey. "Her name is Isabeau of Anjou," he said finally. "Her father, the Comte d'Anjou, was an intemperate fellow who died slaughtering infidels at Antioch. She came to a cousin, I think it was, in Aquila." He was silent again for a moment, looking into the past. A wistful smile pulled at the corners of his mouth. "I'll never forget the day I saw her. It was like looking at . . . at . . ."

Phillipe shut his eyes, remembering. "The
. . . face of love." He smiled, too.

Imperius looked back at him, and his own
smile widened sympathetically. "You too, little thief? Well, I suppose we were all in love
with her in different ways. His . . ." the monk's
throat seemed to constrict, "Grace could think
of nothing else."

Phillipe's eyes widened. "The . . . Bishop . . .
loved her?" he said incredulously.

Imperius nodded, his hands clutching the
tankard's handle in a painful grip. His bleary
eyes turned suddenly bitter. "As nearly as that
evil man could come to the emotion of love. He
was wild in his passion. A man possessed."

Phillipe thought about what he knew of the
Bishop—a holy man who had never known the
meaning of true holiness, who reveled in luxury and sin while he ground the people he had
sworn before God to serve under his heel. He
taxed them until they starved, then hanged them
for stealing food. He was a man with no soul at
all; but even he had recognized the beauty of
Isabeau's spirit, and become obsessed by her
. . . knowing that she was all the things he
would never be.

"Isabeau shrank from his attentions," Imperius
went on morosely. "She sent back his letters
unopened, his poems unread. Her heart had
been lost to the Captain of the Guard."

Realization ran through Phillipe like a shock.
"Etienne Navarre," he murmured. *Navarre*

standing alone with a faded letter in his hands and tears in his eyes . . . Navarre with the wounded hawk. "The madman. . . ." Suddenly he did not seem as mad by half.

"To Isabeau—a fine man, a worthy man," Imperius said sadly. "Their love was stronger than anything which could stand in its way. Until . . ." Imperius broke off again, lifted the tankard and drank as if it were bottomless, or he wished it were.

"Until . . . ?" Phillipe asked impatiently.

"They were betrayed," Imperius muttered. "A . . . foolish priest heard their confessions, and in that priest's subsequent drunken confession to his superior, he . . . felt a holy obligation to unburden himself. The Bishop had refused to let them marry. He had commanded Navarre never to see her again. But they continued to meet in secret. The priest . . ." Imperius broke off again, forced himself to go on, "committed a mortal sin, by revealing their mutual vows of love to the Bishop."

Phillipe stared silently at the betrayer of Isabeau and Navarre. He felt disgust fill him as he watched Imperius take another drink . . . seeing in the old man one more example of the Bishop's web of corruption. But even as he thought it, he knew that he was wrong. Imperius was a deeply religious man. If the fat old monk drank, it must always have been to forget . . . bound to serve the Bishop of Aquila, when he

had vowed to serve justice and truth. But that
still didn't explain why Isabeau, and Navarre—

"He . . . didn't realize what he'd done at first,"
Imperius continued, gazing up at the stars; giving his confession at last to a thief, and to
heaven. "He didn't know the terrible vengeance
the Bishop would take. But His Grace seemed
to go mad—he lost both sanctity and reason.
He swore that if he could not have her, no man
would."

Phillipe's eyes widened again. He leaned
forward.

"Navarre and Isabeau fled from Aquila. But
the Bishop followed them . . ." Imperius told
him everything, his tongue set free by the wine.
Watching the flames, Phillipe saw the tragedy
unfold before him as clearly as if he lived it
himself: the captain betrayed by his own men
on the Bishop's orders; the lovers' desperate
midnight escape from the city, riding together
on the black stallion . . . the Bishop himself
leading the guards in pursuit.

The Bishop followed them, truer than an
arrow, more persistent than a hound, until at
last even the heart of the great stallion reached
its limit. Goliath fell beneath them, and the
Bishop's men closed in like jackals. Navarre
turned and fought. Captor after captor, guards
he had served with, lay dead on the ground.

At last the Bishop, growing afraid for his
own life, called off his men and withdrew. But
he swore that the lovers would never escape

him. Half-mad with fury and frustration, he called upon the powers of darkness. "For the means to damn them, he delivered his own soul to the Evil One. . . ." Imperius shook his head, gazing down.

The wolf's howl echoed out across the valley. Phillipe shivered, not at the sound, but at the power of the evil it had suddenly come to symbolize.

"The black powers of Hell spat up a terrible curse," Imperius said hoarsely. "She was to be a hawk by day, and he—a wolf by night. Poor, dumb animals with no memory of their half-life of human existence. Never touching, in the flesh. Only the anguish of one split second at sunrise and sunset when they could almost touch—but not. Always together. Eternally apart. For as long as the sun shall rise and set. As long as there is night and day."

Phillipe sat stunned and silent, gazing into the flames. At last he pushed himself to his feet and moved away, keeping his back to Imperius, looking out into the darkness in the direction of the wolf's cry. The wolf howled again.

"You have stumbled into a tragic story, little thief," Imperius said. "Now you are lost in it with the rest of us."

Phillipe stood motionless where he was, until he heard the monk's uncertain footsteps retreat into the abbey. He sighed, resting his hands on the solid reality of the low stone wall before

Etienne Navarre (Rutger Hauer) calls the hawk to him, unaware of the hidden Bishop's guards waiting nearby.

A lonely midnight walk with Isabeau (Michelle Pfeiffer) and the wolf.

Navarre and Phillipe ask the Pitous for shelter.

Phillipe rides for the abbey of Imperius with the wounded hawk.

The monk Imperius (Leo McKern) tends the sorely wounded Isabeau.

Phillipe tries to save Isabeau from a perilous fall.

Phillipe and Imperius plan a trap for the wolf.

Isabeau and Phillipe fight to save the wolf from the river's icy grip.

The Bishop's (John Wood) processional in the cathedral of Aquila.

Marquet (Ken Hutchison), the Captain of the Bishop's Guard, rides to the defense of his evil master.

Imperius and Phillipe watch helplessly as Navarre confronts his enemies.

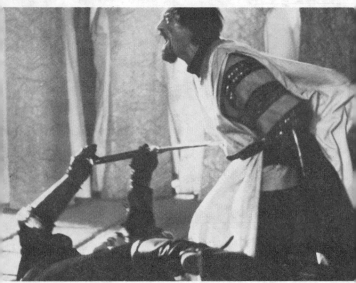

Navarre and Marquet in a struggle to the death.

him. He understood everything now ... even Imperius. He didn't know yet whether he was glad or sorry.

He turned away from the wall, rubbing his arms against the chill that had settled into his bones, and wandered down some steps past a makeshift shed. In the bonfire's dim light, he saw a wooden cage filled with pigeons sitting inside the lean-to. He bent down, peering into the cage. A large white bird stared back at him, cocked its head as if it recognized him.

Phillipe cocked his own head questioningly. "A princess, perhaps?" he asked.

The bird cooed softly.

Phillipe nodded. "Just as I thought. And the rest of you. A sultan's harem?" The birds did not answer. He shrugged. "What the hell. One can't afford to take the chance, these days. . . ." He jerked open the cage. The birds fluttered out in a cloud and flew away into the darkness.

The Bishop stood in the unpleasant and un-accustomed dankness of one of the numberless secret cellars hidden within Aquila Castle. Only one thing could have drawn him to this place in the middle of the night. . . . He gazed darkly at the pile of freshly skinned wolf pelts lying on the floor at his feet. With the toe of his slipper he unlatched the solid-seeming metal base of his clerical staff. It slid back, revealing the gleaming, razor-sharp steel blade hidden within it.

Using the blade's point, he began to peel one pelt and then another off the pile. Each one he saw marked another failure. As the pile continued to shrink, he flung the pelts aside more and more feverishly, spattering his white robes with blood.

The wolf hunter stood to one side, his brutal face filling with fear at the furious intensity of the Bishop's search.

"Useless! All of them!" The Bishop looked up with blazing eyes.

Cezar hunched his shoulders. "My traps are full," he said gruffly. "I can't kill every wolf in France."

The Bishop controlled his rage with an effort, forcing himself to think clearly and dispassionately. There was only one way to be certain that the hunter would find the right wolf. He knew the risk of revealing too much; and yet he had to be sure. . . .

At last he said, "There is a woman."

"Your Grace?" Cezar said, not understanding.

"A beautiful woman. With alabaster skin and the eyes of a dove." Her memory haunted him, night and day. It haunted him now. "She travels by night—only by night. Her sun is the moon, and her name is . . ." Turning back to the hunter, he spoke it like a prayer, "*Isabeau.*"

Cezar continued to gape stupidly at him.

"Find her and you find the wolf," the Bishop

snapped. "The wolf I want. The wolf . . ." he looked on the ghost of another face, "who loves her. . . ." He turned away abruptly, disappearing up the steps.

Chapter Eleven

Day became night and night day for Phillipe and Imperius as they watched over Isabeau. They kept constant vigils at her bedside, but she seldom woke, and was rarely able to speak to them. For the next few dawns Phillipe stood on the parapet above the abbey's gate, searching for a sign of Navarre. Sometimes he called out, telling the silent hills beyond that Isabeau was healing. But he saw no sign of a black stallion or its rider. At first he worried secretly that Navarre might die of his wounds; but each night the wolf was back on the ridge, and he heard its mournful wailing until dawn.

When he was not sitting at Isabeau's bedside, Phillipe wandered through the maze of ruins, unused to having peaceful time on his hands.

The abbey reminded him of the time long years ago when he had been taken in at a monastery and lived with the monks. He had eaten regularly, and they had even taught him his letters, served with heavy doses of scripture; but the rigid discipline and the painful thrashings when he disobeyed had convinced him that he was not cut out for the religious life. With the coming of a new spring, he had run away again. He had never stayed long in one place since, always searching for something that he only seemed to find in dreams.

Phillipe quickly discovered that disillusionment with the religious establishment was the only thing he shared in common with Imperius—besides Isabeau. The old monk treated him rudely at best, and as if he didn't exist the rest of the time, resenting Phillipe's intrusion on his solitude and his self-pity. Phillipe ate the monk's supply of cheese and bread down to crumbs, looked at his books in secret, and ignored the snubs. He had heard far worse often enough, and for far worse reasons.

Phillipe entered Imperius's cell quietly and sat down by Isabeau's bedside as another night began. He looked out at the crescent moon hanging like a jewel in the black sky beyond the window slit, as the wolf's howl carried mournfully across the countryside.

He glanced back at Isabeau as she stirred on

the cot, saw her eyes open, searching wildly.
She tried to sit up, winced with pain.

"Don't!" Phillipe said.

She looked at him, startled and confused.
But her eyes were clear; her fever was gone.
Imperius had told him that since her wound
had not been a mortal one, it would heal with
unusual speed . . . because of the curse.

"You . . . could start bleeding again," he
finished, his voice growing weak as she looked
at him.

She smiled, used to finding him at her bedside by now. "Tell me your name," she said.

"Phillipe, my lady. Phillipe Gaston. Most people call me . . . Phillipe the Mouse." He glanced
down.

"Odd," she murmured. "For one with such
spirit." She took his hand gently. "I shall call
you . . . Phillipe the Brave."

Phillipe blushed. A shiver of astonished delight ran through him. He looked up at her
again with shining eyes.

"You travel with him, don't you?" she asked
softly.

Phillipe nodded, his mind filling with the
heroic exploits of his comradeship with Navarre.
He would tell her how . . .

Isabeau turned her sorrow-filled face away
toward the wall. Her white, slender arms, which
had not felt the sun's warmth in two years,
rested limply on the furs.

Phillipe realized suddenly that what was as

commonplace as waking up in the morning for him was impossible for her ... that she could never ride at Navarre's side, see his face, hear him speak. And in that moment he knew in his own heart what it must be like to live as she had lived—never seeing the sun, or the colors of the day, never holding or even touching the man she loved so desperately. She had been torn from a gentle, peaceful world and thrown into the life of a hunted fugitive ... forced to live with a curse that had stolen away half of her humanity and Navarre's; not knowing if their cursed existence would ever end, or if they would truly live on that way until eternity. ...

Phillipe swallowed the lump in his throat that kept him from speaking. His hands knotted together between his knees as he looked up at her again. Finding his voice, he whispered, " 'You must save this hawk,' he said to me. 'For she is my life, my last and best reason for living.' "

Isabeau stirred, turning her face to him again. Her green eyes searched his own with the fierce passion of a hawk's.

He met her stare. "And then he said: 'One day we will know such happiness as two people dream of, but never have.' "

"He ... said that?" she whispered.

Phillipe nodded. She gazed at him for another long moment, and then at last she smiled, her face brightening with hope and resolution.

She settled back among the furs and closed her eyes, at peace again. Phillipe rose from her side and went quietly out of the room.

Out in the hallway, he pressed his back against the closed door, and sighed. He had been a quick and skillful liar all his life . . . but this was the first time he had ever been proud of it. He smiled with satisfaction and contentment. "Phillipe the Brave," he murmured. And knew that his heart and life were Isabeau's from that moment on, for as long as there was night and day.

Shortly before dawn Jehan led two guardsmen to the crest of another ridge in the endless range of hills. After the latest escape of Navarre and the thief, they had been ordered by the Bishop to continue their search around the clock. Jehan knew that Navarre had been badly wounded—that he could not have traveled far. But they had searched every inch of the surrounding area in vain. Jehan looked down, studying the rocky ground by torchlight for any sign of a trail.

"Look! Over there!" One of his men pointed.

Jehan looked up again. In the distance, silhouetted by moonlight, lay the ruins of an abbey. And below it, the flickering pinpoint of light that marked a fire. Jehan's mouth thinned into a smile.

Phillipe joined Imperius by the garden bonfire moodily. Isabeau's sorrow had become his own, as his heart had become hers. The old monk sat at the table with his tankard of wine, drunk as usual, playing with apples and oranges. Phillipe squatted down on the crumbling terrace. Imperius took another long draught of the wine as Phillipe watched him with sullen eyes. "Does she know?" Phillipe asked at last.

Imperius glanced up at him over the tumbler's edge. "What?" he said testily.

"That you're the priest who betrayed them?" Once Isabeau had known Imperius well, and trusted him far too well. . . .

Imperius hurled the tankard down; it clanged across the cobblestones. "God has declared an end to it!" he shouted. "He has given me the knowledge to undo what I have done!"

Phillipe frowned. "Make yourself clear. If you can."

Imperius struggled to his feet, glaring darkly at him. "For two years I sat here, staring up into the sky, waiting for some indication that my life and service to God hadn't all been wasted and destroyed. The sign never came. . . ." He looked up into the star-filled night. "But I began to see other things."

"Once—when I was drunk—I saw myself as King," Phillipe said sourly.

"Quiet, you wretched illiterate!" Imperius snapped. He turned back to the table and the carefully arranged pieces of fruit. "There are glowing objects in the night sky which seem to be prominent," he said slowly, searching for words to describe a thing that no one had ever described before. "This star here"—he touched an orange—"and the moon . . ." He reached out, then drew his hand back, blinking like an owl. "Where's the moon?"

"I think I ate the moon."

"Fool," Imperius muttered bitterly. He slumped down onto a terrace step, sketching arcs and circles in the dirt with a stick before he looked back at Phillipe. "I have found a way to break the curse. A time for Navarre to face the Bishop and regain what once was his."

"He intends to face the Bishop," Phillipe said. "To kill him with the sword of his ancestors." He got to his feet, remembering that magnificent sword—Navarre's last possession in the world. He understood Navarre's quest all too well, now. He looked out at the night, wondering if Navarre had always hated the Bishop, even when he had served as the Captain of the Guard. His family had given generations of loyal service to the Church. To find himself serving an ungodly tyrant, forced to carry out corrupt and brutal policies in the Church's name, must have been a bitter legacy. Phillipe began to comprehend the true depths of Navarre's hatred for the man who had betrayed his family honor and stolen his rightful heritage from him; whose evil had damned him to an eternity without peace, or hope . . . or Isabeau.

"He can't kill the Bishop!" Imperius said

despairingly. "If he does, the curse will go on forever!"

Phillipe opened his mouth to ask what alternative Imperius really thought there was; then jerked around as a loud banging sounded at the abbey gates.

"Open up in there!" a voice shouted. "Open up in the name of his Grace the Bishop of Aquila!" Phillipe looked back at the monk, stricken. Imperius got to his feet, glancing toward the abbey—toward Isabeau's room—with fear etched into the lines of his face. Then he turned and started slowly down the hill toward the gates. Phillipe followed, his heart in his throat.

Imperius stood at his place on the parapet, looking out and down, while Phillipe crouched beside him. Jehan and two other guards waited below. The two guards carried a heavy log between them; Jehan brandished his torch.

"Go away!" Imperius shouted belligerently, sounding for all the world like a drunken old man. "This isn't a brothel! This is the house of God!"

"Open up for the Bishop!" Jehan answered.

"I've met the Bishop, you blaspehmous lout!" Imperius bellowed. "And you don't look anything like him!"

Jehan turned to his men. "Break it in," he ordered.

Imperius looked down at Phillipe. "Take care of Isabeau," he whispered. "*Run*, you fool!"

Phillipe leaped down from the wall and scurried back up the hill toward the abbey.

The guards ran at the gate with the battering ram. The ancient beam of wood that barred it groaned and cracked.

"By the Virgin," Imperius shouted, "now you've gone *too* far!" He left the wall and started indignantly back up the hill.

Ignoring him, the guards backed away and ran at the door again. This time the entire door ripped from its hinges and fell away under the battering ram's blow. The guardsmen rushed through it and ran up the steps that led toward the abbey garden. The ancient steps crumbled beneath them as they climbed, and Imperius watched in satisfaction as they tumbled back down the hill to the gate.

"Sorry," Imperius called apologetically. "I'm a monk, not an engineer!" The guards scrambled up the rocks again, cursing but undeterred. He stood waiting with saintly patience.

Inside the abbey, Phillipe burst into Imperius's cell. Isabeau looked up at him, fear starting in her eyes. "What is it?"

"Don't talk," Phillipe panted. He held out his hand. She rose from the cot, grimacing, wrapping herself in a blanket. He led her out into the hall, pulling her toward the right. "Come this way."

"Why?" she asked.

He glanced back as he heard the sound of

angry voices. His mouth tightened. "Because I don't think we can go *that* way."

Outside in the garden, Imperius hurried toward the abbey as slowly as he could, urged on by the guards. "Over there, my son!" he said breathlessly, pointing ahead as they started across the drawbridge. "The door on the right! And don't forget . . ."

The guardsman beside him dropped suddenly from sight as the planks cracked and fell out from under him. The guard plunged into the moat with a scream.

". . . to walk on the left side," Imperius finished gently.

Jehan's sword hilt clubbed him from behind, and that was the last he knew.

Phillipe hurried Isabeau through the maze of hallways, trying to keep his growing fear hidden. He had roamed all through this abbey, and he knew that there was just one way out—the way the guards had come in. His only hope for saving Isabeau and himself was to find a hiding place the guards would not bother to search.

He saw the wooden staircase ahead that led up into the abbey's empty, decaying bell tower. It was a poor refuge, but it was the only possibility he could think of. He looked back at Isabeau. "Up there, my lady! Are you able?"

Isabeau nodded wordlessly, her face set with pain. Phillipe took her hand and began to lead

her up the steps. He knew the guards must
have reached Imperius's cell by now and discovered that Isabeau was gone. It was only a
matter of time before they found their way this
far. By then he had to have Isabeau high enough
up that no one would hear their footsteps.

The stairway spiraled up and up, past one
rotting platform after another. Phillipe pulled
harder on Isabeau's hand as she slowed, gasping for breath. He glanced back at her, panic
and concern warring in his eyes, as she stumbled and cried out. He moved down a step to
her side, put his arm around her waist to lend
her strength as they went on climbing. Above
them now he could see the trapdoor that gave
onto the roof. If they could just reach it without being discovered . . .

Jehan halted at the foot of the belfry stairs as
the faint echo of a woman's cry reached him. A
thin smile pulled at his mouth; he gestured
silently. His guardsman started up the steps
ahead of him, sword drawn.

The guard ran up the stairway, moving softly,
peering ahead. As he reached the blind corner
below another platform level, the woman's voice
cried hopelessly, "Please . . . I just can't any-
more. . . ." He grinned and stepped around the
corner.

Phillipe swung around as the guard turned
the corner and thrust his leg between the man's
feet. The guard stumbled off balance; Phillipe

shoved him hard. The guard tumbled down the stairs, falling out of sight with a cry of surprise. Phillipe turned, panting, and looked up. Farther up the stairwell, Isabeau smiled and lifted her hand in a triumphant salute.

Flushed with pride, Phillipe started back up the steps. "Hurry! Keep moving!"

On the landing below, Jehan leaped aside as his guardsman crashed down onto the platform and cracked his head against the wall. Jehan stepped over the guard's motionless body with a curse and ran on up the stairs.

Phillipe heard more footsteps below as he shoved on the narrow trapdoor that opened onto the tower roof. He scrambled through, pulling Isabeau after him, and kicked the trapdoor shut. Searching for some hiding place, they ran out across the ruined roof; but the roof was empty. In the sky to the east the stars were fading, a promise of dawn. They looked down over the parapet, past the jutting gargoyles that leered from beneath the tower eave. Far below, the dove-gray predawn light showed them the jagged rocks of the mountainside waiting like open jaws.

Phillipe looked up at Isabeau, met his own desperation in her eyes.

"Listen," she began in a steady voice, "it's me they want. . . ."

"Don't flatter yourself," Phillipe said grimly.

They turned together as the trapdoor suddenly banged open. Phillipe darted back across the roof as Jehan's helmeted head rose into view. He kicked the trapdoor shut again, knocking Jehan back down into the belfry. Kneeling, he knotted the door's weathered pull rope around a stone cleat. The wood jumped as Jehan began to pound on it with his sword hilt. Phillipe stepped onto the door, holding it down with his weight. He looked again, helplessly, at Isabeau.

Isabeau pressed back against the parapet wall, her face ashen with despair. Suddenly the rotting wood and decaying mortar gave, and a part of the wall crumbled away behind her. Isabeau screamed as she lost her balance and fell backward.

"No! *No!*" Phillipe cried. He leaped across the roof as he saw her fall, lunging after her over the brink. He caught her hand as it slipped from the lip of broken stone, stopping her fall with sheer willpower as her weight nearly dragged him over the edge. He jammed his legs against the wall, bracing himself, staring down into Isabeau's pleading, terror-filled eyes. Then, straining backward with all his strength, he tried to pull her up. But he could get no leverage, frozen against the wall; and he realized, with growing despair, that his arms were not strong enough to lift her weight alone. He could barely even keep his hold on her . . . and that was not enough to save her. Silently he cursed his smallness, his weakness, and the day he was born.

Behind him he heard sudden splintering noises. Jehan banged at the trapdoor with renewed fury as it began to weaken. Glancing back at the sound, Phillipe realized that the air around him was brightening. Sudden hope filled him as he remembered the dawn. He looked down at Isabeau, away again at the horizon, where a pearly luminescence softened the clouds. She twisted her head to look, her fingernails digging into his flesh, her wounded arm dangling uselessly. Day was coming, and with it her change.

But the sun had not climbed above the horizon yet. How long would it take? Seconds? Minutes? If he could only hang on a little longer.... Phillipe bit his lip against the pain. Surely it was getting brighter. He felt as if his arms were being pulled from their sockets. His aching hands were wet with sweat. Isabeau's hand slipped downward half an inch through his grasp ... another half an inch.

Her eyes filled with fresh terror. "Oh, please ..." she gasped.

Phillipe looked away frantically at the horizon. Her hand slipped farther. "I ... can't ..."

Her hand slipped free, and she fell.

"Oh, my God, no!" Phillipe screamed. He flung himself forward, catching empty air. He watched her body tumble down through the growing light—was suddenly struck blind by the first rays of the rising sun.

He flung up a hand to shield his eyes, gaping

in disbelief as a magical transformation began to take place in the air below him. As the sunlight struck Isabeau's body, for an instant time seemed to stop. In that moment as long as eternity, her pale arms blurred and darkened, wideningly amorphously into wings. She seemed to float on the glittering sunlight, her short, streaming hair stiffening into a hawk's crest. . . .

A golden bird hung midway between heaven and earth, beating its wings desperately as it fell toward the rocks below.

At the last possible second, the hawk caught an updraft of warm air. Phillipe sobbed with relief as he watched her feeble wings spread, saw her soar upward on the current, past the bell tower and away into the hills.

Jehan hacked a last chunk of wood from the shattered trapdoor with his broadsword. He climbed through the hole, his sword ready. His eyes swept the belfry roof.

The roof was empty. He circled the tower incredulously, searching for a sign of Navarre or the thief or the mysterious woman who traveled with them. He found nothing and no one. There were no hiding places large enough to conceal even a wounded hawk. He circled the roof again, looking out over the parapet and up into the sky. Beginning to wonder about his own sanity, he turned back to the stairwell at last.

The sound of a piece of masonry dropping

away behind him stopped him in his tracks. He strode back to the wall and peered over the parapet again. Far below him, more bits of masonry clattered onto the rocks. He leaned farther out. Straddling the neck of a gargoyle, pressing back against the wall and doing his best to melt into the stone, was Phillipe Gaston.

Phillipe smiled nervously as Jehan's murderous face glared down at him. "Looks like a nice day," he choked.

"Where's the woman?" Jehan snarled.

"Woman?" Phillipe said.

Jehan's broadsword whistled past his ear, came down on the gargoyle's leering face just in front of him. Chips of shattered stone stung his hands as half its gaping mouth broke away and plummeted to the rocks below. Phillipe's stomach turned over as he watched it fall.

"Where is she?" Jehan asked again.

"She ... flew away," Phillipe whispered weakly.

Jehan's face filled with rage. He raised his sword over his head.

"God's truth, she flew away!" Phillipe shut his eyes in helpless terror. He heard a dull *thunk* above him, and then silence. Forcing his eyes open, he made himself look up.

Jehan stood frozen above him, an arrow protruding from his forehead above his sightless eyes. Slowly he fell forward, toppling over the parapet's edge. Phillipe heard him hit the rocks below a moment later, and grimaced.

Searching the hills, Phillipe's astonished eyes suddenly found Navarre, sitting on the black stallion on a ridge above the abbey. Navarre lowered his longbow. Phillipe sighed, going limp against the stone wall behind him. "It always pays to tell the truth," he muttered. "Thank you, Lord, I see that now...." With exquisite care, he began to crawl back up onto the roof.

Chapter Twelve

Navarre swung stiffly down from Goliath's back as he saw the boy climb to safety. He had not seen everything that had led to this ... but he had seen enough. Looking up, he searched the sky for some sign of the hawk. "Hoy!" he shouted.

Emptiness and silence answered him. The wind whistled along the barren ridgeline. "Hoy!" he shouted again, desperation rising in his voice. The echoes of his call rolled across the land and faded. There was no sign of the hawk. Navarre looked down, sick at heart, turning back to the horse.

A harsh shriek filled the air above him. His head snapped up; he saw the hawk come spiraling down, beating her wings erratically. She landed heavily on his gauntlet, making him wince, and ruffled her wings in recognition.

Navarre stroked her fierce head tenderly, his worried eyes searching out her wound as he murmured, "Shh . . . be still now . . . be still." He held her close to his heart.

The hawk turned her head and nipped him sharply for his overfamiliarity. He jerked his hand away; his mouth twitched with a rueful smile. "So *that's* the way you greet your master, is it?"

He climbed slowly into the saddle again. His healing wounds still caused him considerable pain; but he had known that they were not fatal ones. It was a pain he could endure. And now that the hawk was back in her rightful place on his arm, the truly unbearable pain he had suffered these last days was gone as if it had never existed.

He started Goliath down off the ridge, riding toward the ruined abbey, and Imperius. He had stayed away until now not simply out of physical weakness, but because he had not trusted himself to face his betrayer, knowing that he needed him . . . that Isabeau needed him. But he had kept watch from the ridge, taking cold comfort in Phillipe's shouted reports at dawn, and he knew that this time Imperius had not failed them.

He had had time by now to realize what Phillipe must have been doing at the ambush— that the boy had probably betrayed him, as

well. But Phillipe had more than repaid any
betrayal, by saving the hawk ... by saving
Isabeau.

Navarre rode in through the ruined gate and
up the hill. He stopped before the abbey entrance. Imperius came across the drawbridge
without hesitation and hurried toward him.

Navarre felt his face freeze as he met the eyes
of the man whose weakness had caused so
much suffering, to himself and the woman he
loved. His fist clenched over the reins. Imperius
stopped, seeing his expression. The two men
studied each other for a long moment, face to
face for the first time in two years.

At last Navarre said, "I thought you might be
dead, old man. There were times when I wanted
to kill you myself." He took a deep breath, and
found the strength to say, "I'm grateful for what
you've done here."

Imperius nodded, and looked down. "Vengeance—like forgiveness—is the privilege of
God," he said. "And He has forgiven me." He
sounded as though he actually believed it.

"I am not God," Navarre answered bitterly.
"I have not forgiven you. And I cannot forget."
He dismounted. From the corner of his eye he
saw Phillipe appear at the entrance; the boy
stood watching them silently.

"What will you do, then?" Imperius asked
querulously. "Kill me? His Grace?" He glanced
at the hawk. "Kill her, perhaps?"

Navarre stared at him. "Perhaps."

Imperius shook his disheveled head. "That is not how your story ends! Only *I* know how it ends! God has told me how the curse may be broken!"

Navarre stiffened. His hand shot out, grasping the monk by the front of his ragged robes, pulling him close. "Betray me again, old man?" he whispered, his voice like acid. "Torture me with false hopes?"

With quiet certainty, Imperius said, "Three days hence, in the Cathedral of Aquila, the Bishop hears the confession of the clergy. You have only to confront him—*both* of you, as man and woman, in the flesh, and the curse will be confounded. Broken. The Evil One will seize his prize, and you are free."

Navarre stared at Imperius, searching his eyes for a sign of betrayal or doubt, finding none. It was said that a curse was always imperfect, by its very nature. There was always a flaw, a way it could be broken . . . if the flaw could only be found. "It's not possible. As man and woman. Together in the flesh. Impossible." And yet he had believed it was impossible to escape from the dungeons of Aquila. . . . He glanced at Phillipe, standing mesmerized in the entrance.

"As long as there is night and there is day." Imperius nodded. "But three days hence you'll have your chance. In three days, at Aquila, there will be a day without night, and a night without day."

Navarre stared at the old man a moment

longer, turning the words over and over in his mind . . . feeling the sudden blossom of hope wither and die inside him. His gaze turned as cold as a killing frost. "Go back inside, old man," he said in disgust. "Back to your wine. God has not forgiven you. He has simply made you mad."

Imperius opened his mouth to implore Navarre to listen. But he only shook his head and turned away, unable to face the relentless despair in the younger man's eyes. He started slowly back into the abbey. Phillipe ventured out as the old monk retreated, passing him on the bridge.

Navarre pulled himself together, in control again as the boy stopped before him. He held out his hand. "I am in your debt."

Phillipe shook hands shyly. "Me, sir? Not a bit." He looked up into Navarre's rigidly expressionless face; his own face clouded with concern. "She . . . wanted me to deliver a message," Phillipe said hesitantly. He glanced at the hawk, up again at Navarre. "To say she still has hope. Faith. In you."

Navarre's eyes searched Phillipe's face questioningly, almost ruthlessly; searching for another betrayal. The boy did not flinch or look down. His own eyes shone with belief, until at last Navarre believed it too. With a deep sigh, he looked down at the hawk sitting on his arm. She cocked her head, looking back at him in curiosity.

Phillipe stood where he was, as if he were waiting for something more. Navarre turned back to him again. "You're free to go."

Phillipe nodded. "I know that, sir." He didn't move.

"Do what you like," Navarre said, a little uncomfortably.

"Yes, sir." Phillipe nodded again, hesitated. "Then you and . . . Ladyhawke will be continuing on?"

Navarre looked down at the bird. A gentle, fleeting smile eased his mouth. "Ladyhawke . . ." he murmured. He looked up, remembering the boy again, and the future. "Yes," he said brusquely. "To Aquila."

Phillipe straightened his shoulders. "As it so happens, I'm . . . heading in that direction myself."

Navarre shrugged noncommittally, past caring why the boy suddenly wanted to commit suicide. "Suit yourself." Taking hold of Goliath's reins, he started back down the hill. Phillipe followed at his side, grinning. "Take one of the guards' horses," Navarre said. "You'll tend to the animals as before. Keep a decent fire going. Cook the meals . . ."

"That's my lot in life, sir," Phillipe said cheerfully. "Common as dirt. I cut my first purse when I was seven years old. From a gentlemen going to Notre Dame for High Mass. I thought I'd better get him on the way in, while he still had a few coins left. That night my mother cooked meat for the first time in two years. My family sort of invented poverty, you know, and . . ."

Navarre finally looked back at him again. He wondered briefly whether Phillipe even knew where the lies began and ended in his life. "Still feeling sorry for yourself, eh, boy?"

Phillipe's smile faded. "Born sorry, Captain," he said.

Navarre started, hearing himself called by his old rank. He looked curiously at the boy, trying to read his face.

Phillipe smiled again suddenly. "And sure to die that way."

Navarre laughed, shaking his head.

Phillipe rode out with Navarre into the morning, his head high. He rode his own mount, a fact which no longer terrified him, but only improved his spirits. Phillipe the Brave, Navarre's comrade-at-arms and Isabeau's protector, could handle a horse. And perhaps somehow he might even find a way to change Navarre's mind. . . .

All morning they followed a circuitous route through the foothills, avoiding the Bishop's patrols. The main road to the city was too well guarded now; they would have to find another way to approach Aquila. Navarre stopped for sleep in the middle of the day, exhausted and still weak from his wounds. Phillipe slept beside him, having become a complete partner in the inside-out world that he shared with Isabeau.

By the time Navarre woke, Phillipe had a fire going, and they ate a small meal together. Phillipe had watched the edge of a storm moving in from the west while he waited for Navarre to wake, and as they rode on again, clouds darkened the afternoon sky. Thunder began to roll in the distance. Phillipe put out a hand, waiting for the first drop of rain. "Looks like a big one, Captain. We're going to get soaked."

Navarre glanced up out of his own brooding thoughts and studied the sky between the trees. "Find shelter," he said. "The sun is going down."

Phillipe looked toward the cloud-gray horizon. "How can you tell?" he asked.

Navarre halted Goliath and swung down. "After so many sunsets—how can I not?" He handed his sword, and then the stallion's reins, to Phillipe.

The hawk fluttered down to perch on Navarre's wrist. He held her and stroked her soothingly, then passed her into Phillipe's arms. "Take care of Ladyhawke." He turned and started away into the woods, limping slightly.

Phillipe watched him go with a strange mingling of sorrow and pride. He wondered fleetingly what it would be like to roam the woods all night, a wild beast living on instinct, with all memories of a human existence forgotten. And yet, even the wolf remembered Isabeau,

and the hawk, Navarre. He wondered what
Navarre and Isabeau remembered. . . . He cradled the bird against him, holding the sword as
tightly as if it were a part of his arm. Navarre
stopped, turned to look back at him.

Phillipe grinned confidently, and raised the
sword in a salute.

Navarre returned the salute with a brief smile,
then walked on into the woods. As Phillipe sat
watching, lightning struck a tree somewhere
nearby with an earsplitting crack. Phillipe jerked
around, startled. When he looked back, the
woods were empty. Slowly his frozen smile
came unstuck. His arm trembled with the weight
of the sword; he let it drop with a sigh of relief.

Cold rain began to fall as he rode on. But
before he had ridden far he heard eager voices
and soon saw a group of laughing young villagers hurrying along the road ahead of him. They
were dressed in their festival best and heading
for a small roadside inn. Following them cautiously into its yard, he took thankful refuge in
its vast, moldering barn as the rain began to
come down in earnest. The hawk flew up into
the rafters and settled there, shaking out her
wings and preening. He unsaddled the two
horses and put them into stalls, gave them each
an armload of hay. They shook themselves
and stamped, their breath clouding whitely.

Lightning and thunder cracked and danced.
The rain fell in a silvery sheet beyond the stable entrance. It also dripped insistently though

countless small holes in the barn's neglected roof. Phillipe settled wearily onto a pile of damp straw, Navarre's sword lying safely at his side. Muscles he never knew he had seemed to have been stretched beyond endurance after a day in the saddle. He looked up as the bird fluttered down onto the edge of a stall beside him. "Hungry?" he asked. The hawk looked away. He pushed up onto his knees. "Do you understand me, Ladyhawke?" He watched her golden eye, waiting for a sign of recognition. The bird glanced at him with complete lack of interest. "You know," he went on stubbornly, "it's my favorite thing for dinner, hawk. I've eaten thousands of them. Used to kill one every day, just for practice." The hawk stared at him impassively.

Phillipe shrugged and sat back, hugging his knees, shivering inside his sodden clothes. "Serves me right for getting involved in this nightmare. Nightmare . . ." he muttered. "Daymare . . . and then . . . 'It will be neither night nor day. . . .' " He snorted. "Why not? Makes about as much sense as the rest of it."

He looked up again as the hawk ruffled her feathers. She shuddered restlessly, as if strange sensations were stirring inside her.

Sunset. Phillipe climbed to his feet, feeling sudden uncertainty and distress of his own. Navarre had charged him with protecting the hawk . . . but the hawk was about to turn into a woman. "Listen," he said, feeling his face

redden, "I'll just . . . wait outside, all right?"
He got to his feet and slipped quietly out the
stable door into the darkness.

He huddled under the overhang of the roof,
rubbing his arms and shivering as the rain blew
in on him and his cold, wet clothing became
even colder and wetter. He looked away at the
inn as a cart decked with wedding garlands
pulled up to its door. The laughing, flower-
wreathed bride and groom climbed down, followed by more brightly dressed wedding guests;
together they ran up the steps toward the inn's
entrance. Light poured out into the yard like
warm honey from beneath the inn's covered
porch. Phillipe heard more laughter as the young
couple were welcomed by the crowd of guests
already waiting there. The lilting music of a
lute filled the darkening yard as the celebration
began and dancers chose their partners under
the dripping eaves.

Phillipe stared at the dancers with longing; he
glanced back at the stable entrance. He flexed
his hands as his body began to tingle with
sudden inspiration. Taking a deep breath, he
darted across the yard to the waiting cart, which
was heaped with gifts for the new bride and
groom. Crouching down, he groped among the
covered boxes and bags. After a moment of
searching he pulled out a long homespun gown
dyed sea blue, a rust-colored jerkin, and a linen
shirt. Grinning, he bundled them together and
ran back to the barn.

The hawk still perched uneasily on the edge
of a stall. Phillipe laid the gown out on the hay,
smoothing it with his hands. He glanced up at
the bird. "I can't vouch for the fit, but . . ." He
smiled, embarrassed. "Take your time," he
murmured, and stepped outside into the rain
again.

Navarre trudged through the darkening woods
and the same pouring rain. He followed the
road in the direction Phillipe and the hawk
had taken, staying under cover among the trees;
unable to resist the compulsion that made him
follow, even if he had wanted to. The uncanny
physical sensations of the change grew more
intense throughout his body, the stirring of
strange instincts in his mind grew more insis-
tent, as sunset neared. He pulled off his gauntlets one by one, loosened his doublet; discarding
his clothing, the symbol of his humanity, which
was nothing but an impediment to the beast he
would soon become.

At least this night would be different in one
way from all the nights before . . . at least Isabeau
would not spend it alone and friendless in the
dark. For the first time they had an ally . . . the
unlikeliest one he would ever have expected to
find loyally at his side. An unwilling gratitude
filled him as he remembered Phillipe's farewell salute, and a sharp twinge of hopeless
envy.

Navarre looked behind him suddenly, as his

awakening animal senses told him that he was no longer alone in the forest. He stopped in the middle of a small clearing, searching, listening. A horse was approaching ... two horses ... one man, with the smell of wolves about him— and the smell of death.

A prickle of panic stirred in Navarre's mind as he realized his vulnerability. *Not now ... why did it have to be now?* He started to run, stripping off his clothes with awkward haste. Behind him he heard the hunter ride into the clearing, pull up short as he glimpsed motion. Navarre looked back; for a heartbeat his eyes met the deadly gaze of a man dressed in wolfskin and reeking of blood and he froze. Navarre flung away his shirt and ran on, desperately trying to lose himself among the sheltering trees.

The change caught him in midstride as he fled. A force beyond his control seized him in its supernatural grip, crushing the flesh and bone of a man into the body of a beast, transforming even thought itself. A shimmering wave of dark oblivion swept over him ... and when it passed Navarre was gone. An enormous black wolf bounded on into the trees.

Cezar sat motionless on his horse, staring into the shadowy forest with a brooding scowl of fear.

Phillipe finished changing his clothes beneath the dripping eaves of the barn, humming along contentedly with the music from the inn. He glanced toward the barn doors again, stopped humming as he listened for a voice or sound from within. It was pitch black in the woods beyond the stable; surely it must be well past sunset by now—

"Miss? My lady?" he said softly. There was no answer. "I'm coming in!" he called more loudly, and ducked back inside.

There was no sign of the hawk, or of anyone else, as he looked around the vast, shadowy interior. He listened, his heart beating harder, hearing only the snort of a horse, muted music and the drumming rain. "Miss?" he said again, uncertainly. His voice faded. "Miss, it's me . . ."

Something brushed his arm from behind him. Phillipe yelped and spun around. Isabeau stepped out of the shadows, wearing the gown he had stolen for her. Her eyes were full of gentle gratitude as her hands touched the cloth of her long skirt.

Phillipe swallowed his embarrassment and smiled with pleasure, glancing down. "Phillipe the Brave, remember?" he said hesitantly.

Isabeau smiled in return, like a candle in the darkness, and nodded. She reached out to stroke Goliath's arching neck fondly. Then she looked toward the door, out into the rain and night. "How . . . is he?"

Phillipe raised his head. He said, carefully, "Alive. Like you. Full of hope. Like you."

"He's taking us back to Aquila, isn't he?" she asked.

"Yes." Phillipe nodded reluctantly, and watched a dark foreboding shadow the brightness of her eyes. He took a deep breath and said more briskly, "He left you in my charge, as you can see by his sword over there. 'Tell her we two speak as one,' he said. 'And she will follow your instructions as my own.'"

"Really." She looked up, her mouth twitching as she studied the rafters for a long, thoughtful moment. She looked down at him again finally, and her smile returned. "What . . . do you recommend?"

"I recommend that you sit by a warm fire," Phillipe said firmly. "That you drink a cup of sweet wine, and dance to bright music, cheerfully played." He gestured toward the inn.

"Dance?" she asked, her voice as incredulous as if he had invited her to walk on clouds.

"Why not?" His own smile broke out again. She looked away through the stable door toward the light and music. He watched her face fill with wondering realization, and longing, and doubt—the face of a prisoner who had been shut away in black solitude until even the memory of music and human companionship was no more than a dream to her. The first strains of a new tune drifted in through the open doorway. Phillipe bowed quickly to Isabeau, offering her his hand like a gallant lord. "Shall we practice?"

Smiling with hesitant pleasure, she took his hand and made a graceful curtsy. He put his

arm around her and began to guide her through
the steps and turns of the lively peasant dance.
At first she moved as uncertainly as if she were
dancing on eggs. But each time her feet repeated the steps they grew more confident, until she was whirling as joyfully to the music as
if she had been born dancing. Her pale cheeks
were flushed and her eyes shone; as the dance
ended she turned breathlessly to Phillipe, clap-
ping her hands and laughing with delight.

Phillipe's smile widened as her laughter filled
his ears, more beautiful to him than the music
of a hundred songs. It was the first time he had
heard her laugh; and, looking at her astonished
face, he knew that she was as surprised to hear
that beautiful sound as he was.

Her hands tightened over his, her eyes shone
like emeralds as they filled with unexpected
emotion. He knew that she must have danced
all her life in palaces and manor halls, wearing
gowns of fine silk. But her eyes told him that
none of those moments could ever mean as
much to her as this moment she had just shared
with him.

Phillipe turned away from her, letting go of
her hands, his heart too full; he was suddenly
afraid to test his chivalrous vows any further.
He strode across the barn to the place where
Navarre's sword lay and knelt down to pick it
up.

Isabeau's smile was strangely maternal when
he looked up at her again. "Ah, so you intend

to be my protector as well? I'm flattered."

Phillipe bobbed his head. "In a manner of speaking, my lady. The truth is"—his own smile turned sheepish—"he'll kill me if I lose it." He wrapped the sword carefully in a piece of burlap, to protect it from the weather and prying eyes.

Isabeau picked up a horse blanket and draped it over them both, her eyes alive with anticipation. They slipped out the stable door and ran toward the inn, heads down against the driving rain.

Suddenly a horse materialized out of the darkness; they ran blindly into its side, staggered back in surprise. Phillipe heard Isabeau's gasp as she looked up. He raised his head; forgot to breathe at the sight of the stranger's face.

A huge man with a black beard and scars below one eye glared down at them with the pitiless gaze of a death's head. His face was streaked with blood, which even the rain had not been able to wash away completely. In a thick foreign accent, he said, "Watch where you're going—" as if the next time the mistake might be fatal.

"Yes, sir," Phillipe said meekly. "Thank you, sir." He caught Isabeau's elbow, trying to urge her on. But she stood paralyzed, staring past him, her face filled with horror.

Phillipe turned, and saw what she had seen. The hunter's pack horse was piled high with freshly killed wolf pelts, a ghastly tangle of blood and fur and sightless eyes. Isabeau screamed, and Phillipe drew her to him, holding her in his arms, turning her face from the sight. "Isabeau! Isabeau . . ." he whispered.

The hunter's lips pulled back into a mockery of a grin, showing broken teeth. "Isabeau?" he murmured. "Isabeau. . . ." His grin widened.

Phillipe pushed Isabeau behind him and jerked the covering off Navarre's sword. Raising it with an effort, he pointed the blade at the hunter's face. "Lay one hand on her and you'll find it on the ground next to your head. Now ride on."

The hunter's lips curled with amusement. He reached out in a sudden feint, jerked his hand back as Phillipe slashed at it. "Easy, little man. You wouldn't cut someone for trying to make a living, would you?"

"Are you deaf?" Phillipe shouted. "Ride on!" He pricked the hunter's horse in the rump with the sword point. The animal lunged forward and bolted away, carrying the hunter and his grisly load off into the night.

Phillipe turned back triumphantly. "Well. I guess we showed him what . . ." His voice faded. Isabeau was gone. He looked toward the barn, hearing a noise inside.

Isabeau burst from the stable entrance, riding the black. She dug her heels into the stallion's sides, charging past Phillipe as if he were invisible. He flung himself aside, barely in time to keep from being trampled. She galloped on into the night, following the hunter.

Phillipe picked himself up from the mud and looked out into the empty darkness despairingly. "He'll kill me," he moaned, "he'll kill me!"

Chapter Thirteen

Isabeau rode through the darkness like a madwoman. Branches lashed her face as she forced Goliath through the undergrowth, and her wounded shoulder was on fire with pain; but the only thing that mattered now was the terrible fear inside her. The first gown that she had worn in two years hung on her like a muddy sack, nothing but an impediment. The shining light of the inn, the wonderful promise of wine and song that had shattered only moments ago, seemed to her like a hallucination. This was real—the darkness, the rain, the terror that somewhere in this forest of night the black wolf was in mortal danger.

She slowed Goliath suddenly, seeing something ahead, two blacker shadows against the darkness. She reined in. The wolf hunter's two horses stood tied to a tree in a clearing, their backs turned to the wind. The rain was beginning to let up, and her visibility was slightly better; but there was no sign of the hunter. She rode forward cautiously and dismounted.

A wolf howled somewhere nearby. Her head snapped around; she stared futilely into the gloom. *No! Run! Run!* She wanted to scream it, knowing it would do no good. The wolf was her guardian by night, as the hawk was his by day. It would not leave her. But the wolf hunter had recognized her name . . . and so she knew with terrible certainty what he had been sent here to do. And she knew that this night could end in only one way. Reaching into one of Navarre's saddlebags, she pulled out her dagger.

Clutching the knife tightly in her hand, she started into the trees. She was sure the hunter could not have gone far. He hadn't had the time—and besides, she was sure he would be waiting for them. A dead branch snapped beneath her weight. She froze. There was no answering sound, only the soft patter of water dripping from the leaves. She cursed her clumsiness silently as she started on through the woods. Her father had taught her to ride and hunt like a man . . . but he had never had to hunt by night.

She froze again, suddenly seeing the ghostly outline of another figure just ahead. The hunter was crouched down in a tiny clearing. He raised his head, glancing from side to side like a suspicious animal. She held her breath. But he only crouched down again, for another endless moment, before he rose and disappeared into the darkness.

Isabeau slipped across the clearing, passing the place where the hunter had been crouching. Her foot brushed the edge of the heavy steel trap he had set and hidden . . . and she passed on, unsuspecting, into the trees.

Cezar, who always hunted by night, and had senses as sharp as any wolf's, listened to Isabeau move past his own hiding place. He stepped out from behind a tree and quietly picked up a stone.

Isabeau stopped again, listening, in the eerie, dripping silence. And somewhere in the forest, the black wolf stopped to listen and sniff the air. Steam curled from his nostrils into the chill and damp.

Cezar hurled the stone. It struck the trap behind Isabeau; the jaws clanged shut.

Isabeau spun around in terror, raising her dagger. She peered into the darkness. Silence. Only silence.

The black wolf pricked his ears; he turned and trotted toward the sound.

Cezar hurled another stone. Another trap clanged shut. Isabeau spun back, panting. Silence. "Show yourself!" she cried. Silence. "Coward!" she screamed. Cezar crouched in the underbrush, waiting with merciless anticipation.

Another trap slammed shut, and a wolf screamed in anguish. Isabeau's heart constricted; she stood motionless, paralyzed by the agony of her own horror.

Cezar leaped up from his hiding place and ran to the trap. A large wolf lay dead in it, crushed between steel jaws that had been designed to hold a bear. Cezar grinned in feral satisfaction. He released the wolf's body and pulled it from the jaws; then he reset the trap with deft hands. He started to rise.

Something snarled, directly behind him. He turned, his eyes narrowing. An enormous black wolf stood watching him, its hackles rising. The wolf growled again, baring its fangs.

Cezar spun around, pushing to his feet to flee. Suddenly Isabeau was before him, her eyes dark with vengeance, blocking his escape. She tripped him with her knee and drove him backward into the trap's waiting jaws. The jaws slammed together, choking off his horrified scream.

Isabeau stood where she was, gasping and drained. The wolf stared at her for a long moment with inscrutable amber eyes before it turned and bounded away into the woods. Behind her she heard the loud cracking noises of someone coming heedlessly through the trees. She turned, almost past caring, to see Phillipe emerge from the forest behind her with Navarre's sword in his hands. He stopped, staring in appalled disbelief.

Isabeau started toward the dead wolf wordlessly, passing the hunter's body in the trap. She stumbled suddenly as something caught her ankle. She looked down—and screamed, as the hunter's bloody hand tightened in a death-grip around her leg. He raised his head; his lips pulled back in a snarl of defiance. His face fell forward again, and his hand slid down her foot. Isabeau did not move again for a long moment—could not; her trembling body was utterly strengthless.

Phillipe did not move either, frozen where he stood by his growing realization of all that had happened here.

"It isn't him," Isabeau said dully, as he stared at the wolf. She realized, although it did not matter, that the rain had stopped. A thin fingernail moon winked between the clouds. She looked at the dead wolf silently. She could not tell its color, but it had been a beautiful animal. The trap had destroyed its beauty, its intelligence, its life . . . pointlessly. She glanced at the dead hunter, at Evil struck down by its own tool in fitting retribution. She looked back at the wolf again; she went to where it lay and lifted its broken body as gently as she could, ignoring her own pain. Her eyes filled with tears, but they would not fall.

Phillipe came to her side, his face questioning and uncertain as he looked at the wolf, and up at her.

"I wish it were him," she said, her voice raw.

"You don't mean that, my lady," Phillipe protested softly. "No one can wish for love to die."

She looked back at him, at his boy's face, his mooncalf eyes gazing at her with such shining certainty. Once, she had believed. . . . She smiled bitterly, looking down. "Really?" she said. "And what do you know of love?" She turned away, dragging the wolf's body toward the base of a tree.

"Nothing, I suppose," Phillipe murmured behind her. "I've . . . never been in love. I have . . . dreams, of course," he said wistfully, "but I've never lived the dream."

She glanced up at him. "Then you're a fortunate man." She knelt, laying the wolf's body down beneath the tree. She searched in the leaves for rocks to cover its body with a makeshift grave; she piled them up with sharp, desperate motions as helpless anger rose like a wave inside her. "I've lived the dream and I wish him dead. I wish us both dead. Tell him that." Her voice trembled, as the past two years of living death, the grief and longing and rage that she had held back for so long, suddenly overwhelmed her. "Tell him I curse the day I met him. Tell him, in fact—I never loved him. Tell him . . ." She looked up into Phillipe's eyes, and her own eyes suddenly overflowed with tears. Drowning in grief, she cried, "Oh, how can he go on, day after day, in pain and anguish as great as mine, and still pretend there's an answer!"

Phillipe blinked and blinked, his own eyes full of tears. His hands quivered, as if he fought to keep them down at his sides. At last, in a voice so small she could scarcely hear it, he said, "He . . . loves you."

Isabeau took a deep, trembling breath. She rose slowly to her feet, wiping at her cheeks. She nodded, barely, smiling half in embarrassment and half in profound gratitude at the gift of his words. It was as if Navarre had spoken them himself, they had touched her soul so deeply. . . . She had lived so long in this lonely exile, with her doubt and fear gnawing at her like serpents, poisoning her heart; never daring to set them free, even to speak them aloud, because there had never been anyone to answer them, to deny them, until now. She had not spoken a dozen meaningful words to another human being in two years, until he had come into their lives. . . .

She shook her head as the past rose uncontrollably inside her. She had learned to endure silence, as she had learned to endure the rest, all the things that at first she had thought were unbearable. At first she had left messages for Navarre, and he for her. But as time passed there had been less and less to share, even that way, until at last there was only pain, and even the notes had stopped. Yet even after so long, after so much pain . . . "It's silly, really," she murmured, "but . . . every night, when I wake up, I expect to see him. I know he won't be there, but somehow . . ." She closed her eyes, sighing. "I can feel the tips of his fingers, nestled behind my ear . . . coming down, so." She lifted her own hand. "Tracing the line of my chin . . . touching my lips . . . releasing a smile . . . then covering it with a kiss." She broke off, opening her eyes again. Phillipe's eyes still clung to her face, bright with tears.

"You *have* lived the dream, my lady," he said. "And you will again—if there's a God in heaven." His fists clenched, as if by his own belief he could make it so.

Isabeau reached out, touching his face with gentle fingers, proving his reality. "Even if there is," she said softly, "promise you won't leave us." *Our gift of hope*, she thought.

He quivered slightly under her touch, like a frightened wild thing. "I . . . asked the captain not to rely on me too heavily, you know," he said, glancing down. He looked up at her again, with his cheerful false face on. "I told my mother I'd be back in an hour ten years ago."

Isabeau let her hand fall away, her own smile rueful with understanding. She tried to accept the thought that he might not stay, that tomorrow night she might wake again to years of solitude. Even to have had him here tonight was a miracle. "We've . . . never had someone to help us until now." She looked away, feeling the weight of her burden settle back onto her aching shoulders.

"Don't you worry, my lady," Phillipe said, his voice shaking. "After all—how else can I live the dream?"

She looked up at him, at the tears running unashamedly down his face now, and suddenly her own tears began to fall again. He grinned, and she grinned too, holding out her arms. They held each other tightly for a long time, because they had been such a long time alone.

Chapter Fourteen

Marquet led his men through the ruined abbey by torchlight. Jehan had not reported back, and when they had picked up his trail it had led them here. Marquet stood by the drawbridge while his guards searched the abbey's interior; he was tired and filthy, and his mood was growing blacker by the moment. There was no sign of Jehan or his men, no sign that they had ever left this place again ... but someone else had. He turned back as one of his guards crossed the ruined drawbridge to report.

"Empty, sir. But we found this." The guardsman held up a hawk's feather stained with dried blood.

Marquet squinted at it in the torchlight. A slow, ugly smile formed on his mouth. All his questions had been answered. He looked up at the abbey whose ruins had given shelter to the devil's agent, the Bishop's mortal enemy—and his own. He raised his hand, gesturing at it. "Burn this," he ordered.

They rode out again into the night. Marquet looked back in dark satisfaction as flames consumed the ruins, as the fires of hell would soon consume Navarre.

Navarre strode into the campsite with the new day, looking up into the sky. The hawk soared high in the air, golden in the early-morning light above a snow-capped mountain peak. She came circling down as she saw him and settled onto the lowest limb of a nearby oak. Navarre looked away from her again, without a smile.

Phillipe still slept, as soundly as a child, on the ground beside the dead embers of the campfire; he held the sheathed sword in his arms, hugging it to him like a lover. Navarre felt his mood darken further as he looked at the boy.

He crossed to Phillipe's side and jerked the sword free from his arms. Phillipe woke with a start and scrambled guiltily to his feet. He held his blanket around him, shivering, rubbing his eyes as if he were still exhausted.

Navarre looked at him coldly, then away at the mountain peak gleaming with new-fallen snow. If he rode all day, he could reach Aquila

tomorrow. . . . "All the roads on this side of the
valley are impossible. The only way open to
the city is over the mountain. It will be cold.
There's snow above the timberline." He waited
for the boy's face to fall; waited for him to
begin some excuse, to refuse, to get on his
horse and ride away, and take the sudden un-
wanted burden of his young life with him. But
Phillipe did none of those things; he only stood
looking at him with an uncertain expression.
Navarre turned and moved away toward his
horse.

Phillipe stayed where he was, kicking at the
cold ashes of the fire. "They'll kill you. And
her," he said almost angrily. "You won't get
within a hundred yards of the Bishop."

Navarre hooked his sword over the pommel
and swung up into his saddle. He looked back
at the boy wordlessly, his face set, and dug his
heels into the stallion's sides.

"You should listen to me!" Phillipe shouted,
as he ran to his horse. "I don't *have* to come
along, you know! I'm still a young man! I've
got *prospects!*"

Phillipe caught up with him inside of a quar-
ter mile, and they rode on together. Navarre
ignored the boy for the rest of the morning, as
the horses picked their way steadily upward
toward the pass. The trees began to thin, and
soon they rode along the edge of the snowfields.
The sun shone, making the mountain flash like
silver above them; making Navarre think un-

willingly of his home. His family's ancestral
estates lay peacefully in the mountains five
days journey to the west . . . forever beyond his
reach, now. He urged Goliath on impatiently.

Navarre glanced over at Phillipe for the first
time in hours, as the boy yawned once again.
He had been yawning all morning, and trying
to hide it. "What a night. . . ." Phillipe muttered to himself.

Navarre frowned in uneasy curiosity. "What
. . . a night?"

"Hmm?" Phillipe looked at him, startled. "Oh,
nothing I couldn't handle, Captain." He smiled
pleasantly, pulling the blanket more tightly
around his shoulders, and looked ahead again.

Navarre studied the boy with suspicion. He
looked away and up suddenly, as the hawk
called from high in the air. She had not come
to him all morning, as if she had sensed his
mood. But now she began to circle downward,
and he lifted his arm expectantly.

The hawk flew to Phillipe and landed on his
arm instead. Navarre stared in disbelief as the
boy caught her with an exclamation of surprise.
Phillipe looked up, his chill-reddened face full
of guilt. He smiled feebly, looked down at the
bird again. "Nice bird . . . good little hawk. . . ."
He shook his arm, whispering, "Go to your
master, now." She clutched the thick folds of
his sleeve with her talons. He shook his arm
again. "Go on, Ladyhawke," he said, more
urgently. The bird remained locked on his arm.

She bent her head and gazed at him almost pleasantly. Phillipe squirmed in his saddle under Navarre's withering stare.

"Tell me about it," Navarre said, as they rode on.

"Captain?" Phillipe asked, glancing at him with worried eyes.

"Last night, boy." Navarre forced the words out, an almost-forgotten emotion coiling in his chest like a snake.

"What's to tell?" Phillipe said nervously, looking down at the hawk. "Go on, now. Go, go, go . . ." The bird did not respond. "We . . . ran into a bit of trouble on our way to an inn, and . . ."

"You took Isabeau to an inn?" Navarre's frown deepened.

"Fly to your master—fly to the one you love," Phillipe urged, his distress growing. The bird clung to him like a burr. He looked up again, his face redder with embarrassment than cold now. "Well, you see, first we went to this stable—"

"Stable?" Navarre snapped, running over his words. "What did you do in the stable?"

"We changed clothes, and . . ."

"You changed clothes in the stable?"

"Well, not together, of cour—"

"You left her alone?"

"Never!" Phillipe gasped.

"Then you did change clothes together!"

"No!"

"Don't lie to me, boy!" Navarre jerked the stallion up short, drawing his sword.

The hawk shrieked and fluttered up from Phillipe's arm, settling onto his own. Navarre stared at her, the haze of jealous fury clearing from his brain. Slowly he lowered his sword. To doubt the boy was to doubt her. He had never so much as looked at another woman with any sort of yearning, these past two years, unless the yearning was for Isabeau. He knew in his heart that she had been as true.

Phillipe sighed. "She's the most wonderful woman who ever lived, sir," he said quietly, "and I can't say I haven't had my fantasies. But the truth is—all she did was talk about you."

Phillipe tried to look away; Navarre held the boy's eyes as he sheathed his sword. He left his hand resting on its hilt. "Tell me what she said. *Everything* she said. And I warn you, boy—I'll know if the words are yours." He started his horse forward again.

Phillipe followed, slightly behind, just out of range of Navarre's vision. He heard the boy swallow, as if the words were catching in his throat. "She was . . . sad at first," Phillipe said awkwardly. "She talked about the day you met. She . . . cursed it."

Navarre blinked, as if someone had struck him in the face. His heart sank like a stone.

"And then she said to say she—" Phillipe broke off again. "To say she never loved you." His voice strained.

Navarre looked down at the hawk; she looked back at him with yellow, inhuman eyes. He shut his own eyes against the pain.

"But then she remembered a . . . gesture of yours—the way you had of running your fingers down from the back of her ear . . . tracing the line of her chin . . ."

Navarre opened his eyes to the vision, felt them burning with his unshed tears.

". . . touching her lips . . ." Phillipe went on, with such tenderness that he might actually have known that moment too, ". . . and her eyes glowed—no, *she* glowed—the entire person—as she remembered you . . . 'releasing a smile . . . then covering it with a kiss.' "

Navarre looked down at the hawk again. She gazed into the wind, searching the sky for signs unknowable to a man, while he searched her eyes for the things she would never comprehend. And yet, always the hawk was drawn irresistibly to him, as the wolf was drawn to her. He looked back at Phillipe, his smile filling with sorrow. Even their wild, uncomprehending animal selves were not called to their own kind, but only to a human mate, who could give them no solace. "Did you know that hawks . . . and wolves . . . mate for life?"

"No," Phillipe said. His eyes darkened with understanding.

"The Bishop didn't even leave us that, boy," Navarre said wearily. "Not even that." He looked ahead again, reined in suddenly. His face hardened.

Imperius sat in a mule-drawn cart, blocking the path ahead. His eyes were clear, and perfectly sober. "Still planning to kill His Grace?"

Navarre's hand went to his sword hilt again. "You're the one I ought to kill, old man," he said. "And I will, if you keep following me."

Imperius lifted his head. "Follow me, then. To Aquila. Where two days from now you can face the Bishop in the cathedral, with Isabeau by your side—and watch as the Evil One claims his reward." He turned his mule cart up the slope.

Navarre's hand tightened over his sword. He would not listen—he would not let this guilt-crazed old man ease his own soul by stretching out their agony for even one more day. "I'll be in Aquila tomorrow," he said, his voice as bitter as the wind. "One way or the other—there will finally be an end to it."

Imperius turned to Phillipe imploringly. "Tell him he's wrong! Tell him to give me a chance!"

Navarre glared at Phillipe. The boy looked down at the ground, clearing his throat. "One day more or less . . . what could it matter? Why not give him a chance?" he murmured.

Navarre felt the last small corner of human warmth inside him freeze. "You too," he said in disgust.

Phillipe looked up at him, stung; held his gaze with pleading eyes. But the boy said nothing more, as if he already knew that it was useless. The icy wind whistled across the snow, curling around them like a lash.

"Stay here, then," Navarre said at last. "With the old man. Drink—and delude each other with dreams."

Phillipe shook his head. "I'm coming with you."

"No," Navarre said. He saw the boy stiffen with stubborn defiance. "There will be too many at my front to have to watch my back as well." He wheeled his horse around, so that he did not have to see the stunned hurt that filled Phillipe's face, and spurred away up the hill.

Phillipe sat unmoving on his horse's back, staring down at the snow, his mouth tight.

"You did the honorable thing, little thief," Imperius said quietly. "You spoke the truth."

"I should have known better." Phillipe looked up with bleak eyes, shivering as the wind pulled at his flapping blanket. "Every happy moment in my life has come from lying."

Navarre rode alone, a stark black figure lost in an immensity of white. He was glad to be alone, relieved that he had shaken off the last of the obstacles that stood between him and his fate ... the last of the people who could be destroyed by it. He had lost all control over his life; but at least his death would be his own choice.

The hawk huddled close beneath his cloak.

She nipped his hand in irritation, at the cold and his insistence on taking them through it. He looked down at her, filled with sudden affection and sorrow. At least this was the last suffering he would have to put her through. There would never be another winter of freezing nights without shelter for Isabeau, another spring without the touch of the sun or an autumn without the color of changing leaves. . . . There would be an end to it, one way or another. Their lives were one, and when they died together, perhaps God in His mercy would finally grant them peace, or at least forgetfulness.

Until then, she did not need to know where they were going, or why. Let her be spared that, at least. He looked up again at the fields of snow, and let their blinding glare fill his eyes until he could see nothing at all.

Chapter Fifteen

Phillipe sat beside Imperius in the cart, gratefully wrapped in a sheepskin, as the surefooted mule followed Navarre's tracks through the snow. His own horse plodded behind them, tied to the back of the cart; his stiff legs were equally glad of the change. Navarre would outdistance them today if he didn't stop for sleep. But he would still have to stop for the night. . . . Tonight they would be able to explain everything to Isabeau, and, God willing, make her believe it. Then, even if Navarre refused to listen, together they would find a way to make sure that he had no choice.

He looked up at the ever-rising mountain slope, at the afternoon sun slowly rolling down the sky. Until nightfall, there was nothing to do but follow, and wait. He stifled another yawn and rubbed his eyes. The wind swirled around them again, sending up flurries of white from the snowfields. He looked over at Imperius tentatively, his mind searching for a way to fill the time. "You're a man of science, Imperius. . . ."

The monk sat up straighter. "I like to think so," he said with satisfaction.

"Then tell me: Where does the wind come from?"

Imperius shrugged. "Who knows?"

"And why does the sun make a man's skin dark, but bleach linen white?"

"I haven't the slightest idea." The monk shook his head.

"And where does a flame go when you blow it out?"

"Ah!" Imperius murmured. "Where, indeed. . . ."

Phillipe glanced over at him. "Do you mind my asking you all these questions?"

"Don't be silly, my son," the old monk said placidly. "How else will you learn?"

Isabeau sat listlessly beside the campfire, huddled beneath Navarre's cloak. Beyond the ring of firelight, the frost-haloed sliver of the waning moon bathed the frozen river and its snowy banks with dim blue light. Spare wood lay neatly stacked for her beside the fire, but she had found Navarre's sword lying untended in the

snow nearby when she had entered the camp.
There was no sign of Phillipe, or even his horse,
no second set of tracks leading here. Surely he
could not have left them. She couldn't believe
it, not after last night. . . . Her hands tightened
into fists on the heavy black wool of the cape.

She knew that Navarre was taking them back
to Aquila. But why? Had he finally lost hope?
Phillipe had been evasive and reluctant when
she had tried to press him for details, and her
courage had failed her as she realized what his
reason must be. She could guess easily enough
why he would not answer her. For two years Navarre had haunted these hills, waiting for a
chance to reach the Bishop—to lift the curse
that had been set upon them, or take his revenge for it. But there was no way to lift the
curse; and so there was only one choice left.
And perhaps it was the right one, after all. . . .

Her hatred had never been the same as
Navarre's. She had seen what her father's im-
pulsiveness and ready sword had done to him—
ending his own life, and not the lives of the
enemies of his God. She had not wanted revenge,
at first; she had only wanted to run away. But
she had come to understand Navarre's obsession with staying—for where could they go,
where could they live that would not be a
living hell?

Instead she had turned her own helpless anger in on herself; she had blamed herself for
the Bishop's wantonness, and all the suffering

it had brought to them. In the depths of her grief she had taken her dagger and cut off the golden hair that had once fallen past her waist, that Navarre had loved so much, and left it on the ground for him to find.

But in time she had realized that she was not to blame for the Bishop's lust . . . that only he was to blame. She had gone on cutting her hair short like a man's, because it was more practical, and a useful disguise for an unprotected woman alone. She had learned to live with loneliness instead of despair. And she had grown to understand Navarre's need for vengeance.

The memories of last night flickered in her mind again—the wolf lying dead, the hunter lying crushed in his own trap. . . . *Phillipe*. Where was he? Where? And where was the wolf?

As if in answer the wolf howled, somewhere in the distance. Isabeau's shoulders loosened; she looked out across the frozen river toward the sound.

Snow crunched underfoot behind her. She turned back, startled, to see Phillipe emerge slowly from the trees. She smiled, radiant with relief and joy. "There you are!" she said, trying without success to sound as if she had merely been expecting him. She looked down self-consciously. "It suddenly seemed . . . so different, spending a night without you."

Phillipe stopped, staring back at her for a long moment, as if he could not get enough of the sight of her. Then he glanced down and said, as if he hated the sound of every word, "This may be . . . our last night together, Isabeau."

"No . . ." she whispered, in disbelief and disappointment. She rose from the log. "Why?" She wondered what reason there could be that would not break her heart.

He looked up again, his eyes bright with determination. "There's a chance to break the curse."

Isabeau stared at him, speechless.

"I didn't want to torture you with possibilities," he said quickly, as if he knew what must be filling her mind now. "I didn't want to tell you until I believed—really *believed*—that it could happen. We have a plan. . . ."

"We?" she asked eagerly. "You and Navarre?"

Phillipe suddenly looked very guilty. "No. Me . . ." He glanced toward the woods. "And him."

Brother Imperius stepped out of the shadows. Disappointment stabbed her cruelly. Only that drunken old man, whose weakness had betrayed them . . . who had saved her life, when it could have been cleanly ended.

But he came toward her resolutely, to stand beside Phillipe. "Please, Isabeau, you must hear me," he said. "For Navarre's sake, if not for your own." She looked at the two men, young and old, standing side by side. Their faces swore their belief to her—their wills were united in their need to make her share it.

She nodded, and sat down again by the fire to listen.

She believed them. Phillipe and Imperius went to work, digging out a pit in the solidly packed snowdrift along the bank of the frozen river ... a pit to trap a wolf. The knowledge that they had an ally gave them fresh energy, and soon they had dug down until the icy walls reached above their heads. Somewhere across the river the wolf howled again. Isabeau kept watch, waiting to lure him into the trap when the time came, or lead him away if he came too soon. If they could only keep the wolf—and the man—prisoner for twenty-four hours, then Navarre would have no choice but to arrive in Aquila on the right day.

Phillipe chipped a final chunk of the heavy compacted snow free from the wall with his dagger, sending ice chips flying into Imperius's face.

The monk brushed snow from his hair. "Watch where you're digging, you impossible dunderhead!" he snapped, testy with unaccustomed effort and sobriety. He swung around, knocking Phillipe into the wall of the narrow pit.

"Watch it yourself, or I'll leave you down here for the wolf's dinner." Phillipe picked up the chunk of snow with numb hands and pitched it out onto the pile at the pit's rim. His own fatigue and temper were nearly as bad as Imperius's by now.

They stood side by side, looking up at the slick, icy walls of the pit. Navarre's sword was driven deeply into the snow beyond the pit's rim. Without the rope dangling from its hilt, they would never be able to climb out. Surely it would hold the wolf. He looked questioningly at Imperius, and the monk nodded his satisfaction.

Imperius took hold of the rope, testing its strength. "Me first." He grasped the rope. "You'll have to push." He began to pull himself upward with a gasping effort, his feet planted against the wall.

Phillipe pushed dutifully, grunting, "When you kneel before the altar ... how do you get up again?"

Imperius frowned darkly over his shoulder as he heaved himself up out of the pit. He lay panting in the snow as the wolf howled again. The sound was louder than before. "Quickly!" Imperius whispered. "He's coming!"

Phillipe caught the rope and scrambled up out of the hole. He got to his feet and shook ice chips out of his clothes; pulling Navarre's sword from the snow, he drew the rope up out of the pit. Isabeau stared out across the river. The wolf called again, closer now. She glanced back at them, with sudden uncertainty in her eyes as she faced the moment of betrayal.

"It's the only way," Phillipe whispered. "Do it!" He circled the mound of snow they had made beside the pit and lay down flat on his stomach, the sword at his side. He tossed back handfuls of white powder to cover his legs. Imperius lay down heavily next to him and did the same.

Watching Isabeau from their hiding place, they saw her stiffen as she caught sight of the wolf. It came trotting up the snowy hillside from the distant timberline; it stopped, sniffing, searching the air for her scent. Isabeau stepped out onto the frozen river, trying to draw its attention. The ice creaked under her feet. The wolf pricked its ears, looking toward her. It started forward again, loping up the hillside; halted as it reached the far side of the river. Isabeau halted too, glancing down uncertainly at the ice beneath her feet. She looked up again, held out her hands.

"That's right, Isabeau," Imperius whispered. "Lead him to the pit. . . ."

The wolf started out across the ice. Phillipe heard the ice creak with his passage. Sliding and slipping as his feet lost traction on the slick surface, he came to her, drawn by an urge as irresistible as it was forever incomprehensible to him.

Isabeau backed cautiously toward the shore, her eyes always on the wolf as she drew him toward the pit. He followed her step by step. Suddenly Isabeau stumbled; Phillipe heard her gasp as her foot went through the ice. He pushed himself up, watching wide-eyed as she caught her balance and scrambled frantically back toward the bank.

As the wolf saw her stumble and the ice break, he bolted forward, running to her as she fled toward safety. Abruptly the ice gave way beneath him, and a vast black pool opened and swallowed him up. Isabeau spun around as she heard him fall through the ice. She ran heedlessly back onto the frozen river.

"Oh, my God!" Phillipe pushed himself to his feet, grabbing up Navarre's sword and the rope. He vaulted over the pile of snow and ran toward the shore.

The wolf broke the surface of the water, thrashing wildly as he clawed at the icy rim of the pool. He sank from sight again. Isabeau lay flat at the edge of the hole and plunged her arm into the freezing water. Catching hold of a fistful of fur, she pulled with all her strength. The wolf's struggling, submerged body dragged her own body forward over the slick ice to the rim of the hole, but still she did not let go.

Phillipe threw himself down at the edge of the river and clamped his hands over Isabeau's ankles. He pulled her back from the brink with the strength of desperation. But his own feet lost all traction as he pulled harder.

The wolf surfaced again, snarling in confusion and pain, dragging them forward again. Phillipe began to slide with Isabeau, back toward the water. Suddenly Imperius was beside him, his own hands circling Isabeau's feet, stopping the slide with his greater weight. "Help her!" he shouted at Phillipe. "Get him out!"

Phillipe got to his feet, helplessness filling him as he watched the wolf's panic-stricken struggles. Suddenly he remembered Navarre's sword still lying behind him. Turning back, he lifted it with both hands and drove it into the ice. Fractures spread from the impact, but the ice held. The wolf sank again. Phillipe caught up the end of the attached rope and leaped into the water.

The black, icy river closed over his head. He fought his way back to the surface, gasping with the agonizing cold; found himself face to face with the snarling wolf. The wolf lunged at him, its eyes wild with fear, its claws ripping his tunic. Phillipe floundered, hanging on to the rope. Somehow he got a loop of it over the wolf's head, and then another.

As the wolf felt the rope tighten around its throat, it lunged at him again in a frenzy. Its fangs ripped his shoulder, its claws raked his chest. Phillipe screamed with pain, and sank. He struggled back to the surface desperately, clinging to the rope like a lifeline, and dragged himself up out of the hole before the drowning wolf could attack him again. Staggering to his feet, he pulled on the rope with all his strength.

The wolf broke the surface once more, choking and gasping for air. Isabeau seized the ropes around its neck, and together they hauled the animal inch by inch out of the water and onto the ice.

Phillipe fell to his knees, dazed with pain and shock. The wolf lay on its side, shuddering with cold. It tried once to get its feet under it; collapsed again, its flanks heaving. Isabeau stroked the wolf tenderly, reassuringly, as she uncoiled the rope. She buried her face in the wet, icy fur of its shoulder. The wolf lifted its head, panting, its eyes rolling to stare at her. Its head dropped back and it lay still, exhausted.

Phillipe lay where he was, as utterly spent as the wolf. Imperius came to his side, pulling him to his feet, helping him toward the shore. Isabeau looked up at them, her face filled with anguish too deep for words. Her eyes burned with resolution as she gazed at Imperius. "We must live, Father," she whispered finally. "As human beings. Our lives are in your hands, now."

Chapter Sixteen

Phillipe woke out of an exhausted, nightmare-haunted sleep as the sky began to brighten in the east. He rolled over, away from the light, gasped out an oath as the pain in his chest and shoulder startled him awake. He lay back, staring up into the brightening sky as he tried to remember what had happened to him. *The wolf.* He pushed himself up cautiously, grimacing. *Isabeau* . . . He found her lying near the fire, just as he remembered, asleep beside the wolf beneath Navarre's heavy cloak.

But as he watched, the first rays of the morning sun flashed above the horizon. The light of the new day flowed across the snow and lit their peaceful, sleeping forms. They woke together, suddenly, as the metamorphosis be-

gan inside them. And caught inside that time-
less instant of change, Isabeau and Navarre came
face to face in the flesh.

Isabeau reached out as the wolf's face shimmered, becoming Navarre's. Her fingers stretched
toward him—spreading, changing, becoming a
feathered wing. The wolf shuddered, his spine
unbending, his clawed foot lengthening into a
human hand and fingers. Navarre reached out
to Isabeau, as her yearning eyes narrowed, hard-
ening into the cold, penetrating stare of a preda-
tory bird. Navarre moaned in anguish, as his
hand closed over emptiness, and his lover van-
ished before his eyes.

Navarre slumped back beneath the cloak as
the hawk spread its magnificent wings, taking
off into the sky. Phillipe bowed his head, aching with their sorrow, and his own.

Navarre sat up slowly, pulling on the clothes
that Isabeau no longer needed, his face drawn.
Phillipe untangled himself from his blankets,
already dressed in the dry clothing Imperius
had forced his shivering body into last night.
He heard the monk stir and wake behind him
as he shuffled toward the dying campfire.
Grimacing, he bent down stiffly for an armload
of branches to build up the blaze. Imperius
had poured half a jug of wine over his wounds
and down his throat as well last night, and he
supposed that he would live. But he didn't
expect to enjoy it much for a few days.

Navarre got to his feet, looking around the

campsite with an unreadable expression. If he wondered how the wolf had come to be sleeping beside Isabeau, he did not ask. His eyes flicked past Imperius, dismissing him, and settled on Phillipe. Phillipe held his breath. "My sword," Navarre said.

Phillipe straightened up from the fire, his stomach knotting with anticipation.

"Where is it?" Navarre asked harshly, when he did not answer.

"Gone," Phillipe said, meeting his eyes. "It . . . fell through the ice last night . . . crossing the river."

Navarre's face filled with incredulous loss. "Damn you! Damn you to hell! That sword was mine from my father and three fathers before him! The last bit of honor I possessed!" His voice shook. He looked toward the river and back again murderously.

"I can't undo it!" Phillipe shook his head, his own voice sharp with tension. "But don't you see? There is no mission of honor now. No jewel to be stuck in a sword hilt as a symbol of your meaningless death!" Navarre's expression did not change. Desperately, Phillipe said, "But there's a chance for life! A *new* life! With *her*, if you will only listen to us!" He held out his hands.

Navarre glared blackly at him, at Imperius. "I don't need a sword to kill the Bishop." He turned away toward his stallion.

"Navarre . . . Navarre . . . don't go!" Imperius cried. Navarre did not even look at him.

Phillipe crossed in front of the monk, blocking Navarre's path. "Go ahead then," he said fiercely. "Kill yourself! Kill *her* too! You never cared as much for her as you did for yourself anyway!"

Navarre lunged at him with a curse. Phillipe dodged, not quickly enough. Navarre's fist closed on his shirt, ripping the worn cloth, as Phillipe lost his balance and fell backward.

Phillipe lay panting in the snow, giddy with pain. Fresh blood oozed from the wound on his shoulder and trickled warmly down his side. He pushed himself up onto his elbows, looking down at the rags of his shirt, at the livid welts and gashes on his bare chest. He looked away again hurriedly.

Navarre stood motionless above him, staring down at his wounds in disbelief, like a man reliving a dream.

Imperius rose from his blankets. "It . . . happened last night. While he was saving your life."

A tremor ran through Navarre. The rage drained from his face; sorrow and shame replaced it. He turned away abruptly from the sight of what he had done.

The hawk swooped down in front of him, landing on Goliath's saddle. She cocked her head at him questioningly. Navarre gazed at her for a long moment before he turned back again to Phillipe.

Phillipe got to his feet, pulling the rags of his shirt together.

"Forgive me," Navarre said softly.

"I can't." Phillipe shook his head, looking up.

Navarre blinked in surprise. A frown of dismay creased his forehead as he searched Phillipe's dark eyes for something he was suddenly afraid he had lost, or destroyed.

Phillipe let the corners of his mouth curve up in a tiny smile. "It's not my place, sir," he said with a shrug. "I'm as common as dirt, just like my mother said."

But Navarre did not smile. Instead his own eyes filled with sudden emotion. "Your mother did not know you as I do," he said, his voice husky.

Phillipe glanced down, unable to face what he saw in Navarre's gaze. A feeling he could not even put a name to filled him until he could barely speak. But he forced the words out. "My mother did not know me at all, Captain. She died two days after I was born— hanged for stealing a loaf of bread." He listened with a kind of disbelief to his own voice telling the truth. Raising his head again, he said, "I . . . wasn't trying to be a hero last night, it's just that . . . I . . . never had a friend before."

Navarre's arms reached out and pulled Phillipe to him in a gentle bear hug. Phillipe grinned, holding on, all pain forgotten.

*   *   *

Navarre stood looking down into the hole that Phillipe and Imperius had dug to trap the wolf. They had told him haltingly about last night, of their absurd and nearly fatal attempt to capture him. He looked back at them again, raising his eyebrows. They stood before him with heads hanging like guilty children.

"We hoped to . . . reason with you," Phillipe said in a small voice, daring to look up at him again.

Imperius nodded. "At the very least—to make sure you didn't arrive in Aquila until tomorrow, when the time will be right."

Navarre studied their determined faces, feeling as if he actually saw clearly for the first time in years. What Imperius claimed was sheer insanity—and yet . . . "You both believe . . . enough to do this?" He gestured at the pit. The hawk circled down to him, settling on his wrist.

"To tell the truth, sir, we didn't know *what* to do," Phillipe said. He glanced at the hawk. "Digging the pit was her idea."

Navarre looked at the hawk, surprised, and yet somehow not surprised at all. "Three against one, is it?" he said, resigned. The bird looked at him uncomprehendingly. She spread her wings, launching off into the sky again. He watched her fly, awed as he always was by her grace and strength, the beauty and freedom of her flight. And yet always she returned to him, because the bond they shared was stronger than instinct, or life itself.

He looked down again. He must truly have been mad, to have been so blind—to surrender to the Bishop's evil, to willingly throw away their lives. He could not sacrifice her life, or even his own, on a useless, suicidal vendetta, as long as any hope of breaking the curse remained, no matter how small—or how insane.

He glanced into the hole again, for a brief moment picturing himself there, a snarling animal trapped in a pit. It was what he had become by day as well as by night, these past two years. But no longer. His mind was free—and suddenly it showed him the flawless disguise that would take him past the walls and the guards, and into Aquila alive. A disguise as much a part of him as his own skin. . . .

He looked back at Phillipe and Imperius. "Then let me show you hopeless idiots how to trap a wolf."

The monk and the boy gaped at him, then looked back at each other in astounded relief, as they realized that they had won.

They worked through the morning under his direction, cutting branches to construct a cage, lashing them together with pieces of torn blanket. At last he was satisfied that they had a trap no wolf could escape from . . . not even himself.

They loaded the cage onto Imperius's cart, and traveled on down the mountainside until they reached the foothills overlooking the city. There they made camp for the last time, waiting for sunset. As the evening drew near, Navarre hid his saddle and weapons beneath Imperius's belongings in the cart and hitched Goliath to its traces.

Then he left the others, to stand alone on the sheer stone precipice, gazing down at Aquila, as he had stood and studied it through countless days during the past two years. This time, at last, the city walls did not look impenetrable or the towers of Aquila Castle as unreachable as heaven. The hawk launched from his wrist into the air, stretching her wings in one last flight before nightfall. He watched her fly with an ache in his chest, and started back to the camp.

He looked down at the cage sitting on the ground by the fire . . . waiting for him. He sighed. "So much has to go exactly as planned—and nothing in my life ever has." He faced the others: Imperius, who had betrayed Isabeau and himself out of weakness, but who stood ready now to give up his own life if necessary to save them. And Phillipe, ready to risk his life for them for a reason that was even more extraordinary and rare. This might be the last time he ever saw either one of them. . . .

He let his eyes record every detail of their faces. "If you should be the ones to survive," he said softly, "think well of me. And if God has chosen to sacrifice us all—He has blessed me with the two most loyal friends a man ever had."

A shriek filled the air above him as the hawk

swooped down to his arm. He caressed her gently, his eyes blurring until she seemed to glow inside a halo of light. "We have known true love, Isabeau," he whispered. "No one could ask for more."

Chapter Seventeen

Blazing campfires lit up the moonless night before the walls of Aquila. Marquet had ordered his men back to stand guard in force before the city gates, as clergy gathered from miles around to give their confessions to the Bishop. Navarre was still at large, and the Bishop's mood on this eve of the holy day was distinctly unforgiving. Marquet knew, as His Grace did, that the influx of strangers offered Navarre a perfect opportunity to slip into the city. And Marquet knew, as the Bishop did, that his life depended on seeing that it didn't happen.

The guardsmen huddled close to the campfires among their tents, trying to keep the night's chill away, as countless abbots and abbesses,

priests and friars and nuns, made their way
through the encampments toward the arching
bridge and the well-watched gates of the city.

Imperius sighed heavily, releasing his held
breath at last as he guided his cart along the
Aquila road through the encampments. Isabeau
sat beside him, wearing a monk's robe, her face
hooded by the cowl. As he had hoped, no one
gave them more than a cursory glance as they
approached, two among so many religious
pilgrims. Most of the glances went to Navarre's
stallion, docilely drawing the cart. In the back
of the cart, the wolf lay silently in its cage,
hidden beneath a blanket. And beneath the cart
Phillipe lay hidden too, waiting for the moment when he would slip away to play his
own role in their plan.

"God's mercy . . . God's mercy. . . ." Imperius
greeted the guards warmly, lifting his hand to
bless them, as the cart passed through another
camp, the final one before the city gates. Isabeau
glanced nervously at him; he nodded in placid
reassurance, wishing silently that he had not
given up the last bit of his wine.

As they approached the bridge he slowed his
cart, allowing other pilgrims to pass ahead of
him; allowing Phillipe a moment in the shadows and confusion to drop from beneath the
cart and disappear under the bridge's arch. Then
he drove on, with his heart in his throat, watching the gates loom above them.

A huge, surly guardsman stepped out in front of the cart, raising his hand. Imperius stopped the stallion obediently. The guard circled them slowly, peered with suspicion at the covered cage. Imperius took a deep breath. "A surprise gift for His Grace, my son. From the devoted people of my parish."

The guard ignored him, and reached into the cart abruptly to jerk away the blanket covering the cage. The wolf snarled and sprang to its feet, snapping at the guard's hand through the cage bars. The guard leaped back with a startled grunt.

"A fine pelt for his wall. . . ." Imperius murmured as the guard came forward again, his suspicious eyes now peering at the cart's human occupants. He stopped beside Isabeau, who sat slumped over, her face hidden beneath her hood.

". . . A luxurious rug for his floor . . ." Imperius droned on, with an earnest smile. The guard reached up and peeled back Isabeau's hood. She jerked around, her face filled with fear. Imperius felt her shudder as the guard leered at her.

"A . . . most pious daughter of the Church," Imperius said hastily. "Poor thing's deaf and dumb. Excuse her nervousness. It's her first time in Aquila."

The guard's malicious grin widened. "Deaf and dumb, eh? That's how I like them too, Father. . . ." He reached up. touching her cheek with a filthy hand. She flinched away in disgust.

The wolf lunged against the cage bars with a furious snarl. Its paw shot out; claws raked the guard's exposed arm.

The guard leaped back, his face filling with fury. He drew his sword, his mouth pressed tight. "I've never had the pleasure of killing a wolf before," he muttered.

Isabeau gasped. Imperius caught her arm in painful warning as she would have thrown herself off the cart at the guard. "Odd," he said loudly, "that's precisely what *His Grace* said."

The guard froze and looked back at the monk with an uncertain frown.

"When he heard about the gift," Imperius bent his head at the cage. " 'I've never had the pleasure.' " He shrugged. "But I'm sure he'll understand you had your reasons. He's a notoriously forgiving man."

The guard hesitated, looking back at the wolf. He lowered his sword truculently, his frown deepening. "Pass on through, Father."

Imperius clucked to the stallion and started on. "May God grant you your just reward, my son."

Watching from the shadows below the bridge, Phillipe sighed as he saw the cart pass safely through the gates at last. "We've come full circle, Lord," he murmured. "I'd like to think there's some higher meaning to all this." He looked up at the sky. "It certainly would reflect well on you." He removed the coil of rope from beneath his tunic, checked it carefully before he slung it over his head and shoulder. Then, taking a deep breath, he slipped into the chill black waters of the moat.

He swam toward the grating he had escaped through only days ago . . . days that seemed somehow to have become a lifetime. Fighting the current of the outflow, he caught hold of the grating. He took a deep breath, and then another, with a fervent prayer that this was not about to become a lifetime literally—a painfully short one. Holding his third breath, he ducked under the surface.

He pulled himself downward along the grate, battered by the cold, surging water. His hands felt their way to the gap between the bars at the bottom of the grating, and he dragged himself under it. The current pried at his fingers, nearly sweeping him loose and carrying him away over and over again, as he squirmed like an eel past the clog of debris trapped behind the grate.

He shot to the surface again, gasping for air in the reeking darkness. He was inside the walls. He climbed up the slippery grating, more grateful than he had ever expected to be that he had already done this once the hard way. Flopping onto the ancient access ledge carved into the tunnel wall, he huddled there, feeling for the flask of wine that Imperius had given him to warm his shivering, aching body. He would have to wait for dawn, for enough light to filter

down into the caverns to let him find his way
back to the cathedral. He took a long swig of
wine and sighed, promising himself that at least
the hard part was over. . . .

Imperius and Isabeau exchanged smiles of
heartfelt relief as they drove through the dark,
deserted back streets of Aquila, searching for
the unobtrusive alleyway Imperius had chosen
as their hiding place while they waited for the
new day. At last they reached the quiet cul-de-
sac, surrounded by windowless walls and piles
of hay from a nearby stable. Imperius halted
Goliath with a nod of satisfaction. He looked
up at the narrow slice of sky between the
buildings, where, in the morning, they would
see . . .

His smile faded. Overhead the stars were disappearing one by one behind a spreading edge
of clouds.

Chapter Eighteen

The new morning brightened over Aquila, revealing a sky entirely gray. The cathedral bells began to toll, rousing believers and nonbelievers alike, reminding them that this was the day of atonement. Marquet paced the broad, curving ramp that led to the cathedral entrance, staring out across the deserted square as if by sheer will he could make Navarre appear. He was ready; he had been ready for far too long, by now. He ached for this. They had found no trace of Navarre last night; nothing even remotely suspicious had been reported. And yet Marquet was certain that Navarre was here . . . just as certain as he was that he would be the man to kill him.

* * *

The Bishop moved restlessly about his bed-chamber, twisting the emerald ring on his thumb. Navarre was trying to come for him, mad with revenge; he was certain of it. Everything and everyone he had sent against Navarre had failed. It was almost as if Navarre were under some sort of divine protection. . . . And yet, what did he have to fear? There was no way his former captain could possibly get past the ring of guards with which he had surrounded his city and himself. And there was no way that Navarre could break the curse. His own soul was safe from hell, as long as Navarre was damned . . . Navarre, and Isabeau. . . .

The Bishop reached out, distractedly picking a sweetmeat from the silver platter on the filigreed table below the window. He looked out at the sky, gray again with clouds. It had rained almost every day in the past two weeks . . . ever since that wretched thief had escaped from the dungeons. Perhaps the drought had ended at last. Crops would be good in the coming year. Surely it was a sign that he had nothing to fear. This time, when he raised the taxes, the people would pay. . . . He licked his lips.

A knock sounded at the door. He turned back from the window, glancing toward his bed. His mistress sat up among the silks and furs; she rose from the bed like a sleek cat at his gesture. Slipping into a robe, she disappeared through a doorway into another of his private chambers.

"Enter," the Bishop said. Two acolytes entered the room reverently, carrying the heavy, lace-trimmed brocades and satins of his robes for the Mass.

The cathedral bells continued to ring out across the city as the morning brightened. Imperius stood beside his cart, looking up. "Perhaps one hour, more or less," he muttered, speaking to the air and hoping for an answer. "Who can tell, with this sky?" He pulled his cowl up under his chin, shivering with the chill as he gazed nervously at the clouds. From his observations through endless nights and seasons, he was sure that what he believed would happen could only happen today. But if they could not see the sun, how would they be able to tell when it was beginning?

P'dee— The hawk's cry reached him from far overhead, and he glanced up again.

Navarre moved out from behind the cart, looking up with a frown as he pulled on his gauntlets. "Hoy!" Navarre shouted. He watched the hawk wheeling in the cloud-filled sky high above. She soared away over the thatched rooftops of the town. He looked back at Imperius, his frown filling with concern.

"She'll be back," Imperius said, never doubting that the bond between them would hold. "Gaston's the one I'm worried about."

"I trust him." Navarre shook his head, unconcerned.

Imperius hunched his shoulders skeptically.

The boy was like quicksilver. When it came to actually risking his life, how sure could they be of his loyalty? "If he made a run for it last night when he had the chance, you're a dead man," he muttered.

Phillipe stirred on the ledge as he realized that he could actually see his hands in front of his face. He drank the last swallow of wine and climbed to his feet. Daylight seeped through the clogged grating; more light shafted down into the underground deeper in the sewers. He stretched his aching, reeking body cautiously and began to feel his way along the ledge, back into the caverns. It occurred to him that he had been born in a prison, and now he was likely to die in a sewer. He grimaced, muttering, "I should have made a run for it when I had the chance. . . ."

Marquet left the cathedral steps and crossed the square. A mounted troop waited for him— the best of his men, the honor guard that would escort the Bishop and the clergy to services. Grimly he mounted his gray stallion and led the troop away toward Aquila Castle.

The castle's gardens were already filled with the elite of the gathered clergy. Priests and friars, monks and monsignors clustered together in groups like exotic birds, clad in their finest robes. Some stood with heads bowed, murmuring prayers, while others idled over bowls of

fruit and trays of delicacies, tittering at the
latest gossip.

A sudden silence fell over the courtyard as
the Bishop stepped out of the atrium, a dazzling figure in white and gold. The gathered
clerics turned as one to acknowledge the ar-
rival of their spiritual leader. He paused a
moment, studying their attentive, nervous faces,
before he lifted his hand, in a benediction that
had more the feeling of a threat. The watching
clergy genuflected hurriedly, already counting
their sins.

The Bishop passed among them, nodding right
and left as he gestured the crowd together for
the procession. Several friars gathered about
him, raising a crimson canopy over his head.
He led the train of his followers to the garden
gates, where Marquet waited with the honor
guard—still captain, but only by the grace of
God. The Bishop acknowledged him coolly.

The clergy assembled behind the Bishop, gathering in order of rank from richly clad monsignors to humble nuns and friars. The massive
gates of Aquila Castle swung open, and the
procession moved out into the streets, flowing
through the city in a splendid display before it
turned back toward the cathedral. The citizens
of Aquila lined the way or hung out of windows to watch the procession pass. The richness of the robes, the bright banners and gilded
crosses, the censers filling the air with per-
fumed smoke, were far more beauty and pag-

eantry than most of the watchers had seen in a
year. The chanting of the clergy and the ringing
of the cathedral bells filled the air with unaccustomed music.

To Phillipe, the sound of bells and the pag-
eantry in the city streets up above him seemed
considerably farther away than the gates of
paradise. He dragged himself inch by treacherous inch up the shaft that opened into the
cathedral, threading the rope he had tied around
his waist through the rusted iron rings as a
safety line while he climbed.

He stopped halfway up the shaft, breathing
hard, clinging to the rope as he dared to look
up again. He saw the rose window high above
him like a vision, a sudden blinding flash of
brilliance and darkness that assaulted his eyes,
just as he had seen it once before. He blinked
his eyes, and its colors came into focus. But as
he remembered what had brought him back to
this place, the glowing illusion of black and
white seemed to symbolize a promise. *A day
without night, a night without day.*

He pulled himself painfully up the last few
feet and tied off the rope at the highest ring,
freeing his hands for work. He pulled his dagger from his boot and began to pry at the eroded
metal bolts that held the grating in place.

Navarre and Imperius listened as the sounds
of the procession grew louder and then grad-

ually faded away, heading toward the cathedral. Navarre stared at the sky, where a perfectly normal day was proceeding behind a perfectly impenetrable blanket of clouds. He looked down again, his jaw set, and moved restlessly to the stallion's side. He began to unfasten the traces that held the horse to the cart.

Imperius glanced up at the clouds nervously, seeing Navarre's agitation. "It should be soon now. Once these clouds break . . ."

Navarre pulled his saddle from the cart and turned to face the monk. "It's day, old man. All day. As it was yesterday, and as it will be tomorrow, if God grants me the life to see it." He settled the saddle on Goliath's back. Imperius looked down at the ground wordlessly.

Beyond the warren of buildings that separated them from the cathedral, the procession of penitent clergy wound slowly into the open square. The mounted guard troop fanned out before the cathedral entrance, sitting at attention as the clerics passed between them and up the broad ramp. The Bishop glanced at Marquet as he passed, and the look in his eyes was far from a blessing. Marquet nodded imperceptibly.

Just within the cathedral, Phillipe worked the last bolt of the grating loose. It fell through the grate, tumbling past him down the shaft into the darkness. Elated, he pushed upward on the grate, felt it begin to rise.

A cavernous thud echoed through the cathedral, as the massive, carven doors swung open.

The sound of chanting filled the vast hall, and the procession of clergy began to enter.

Phillipe saw the Bishop silhouetted in the sudden light of day, his figure dwarfed by the immensity of the cathedral's arching entrance and the vast wooden doors. Phillipe ducked back into the shaft, letting the grate down over his head with a silent curse of frustration.

In the hidden alleyway, Navarre slipped the bit into the stallion's mouth, pulled the bridle into place with fatalistic calm. The hawk perched on his saddlebow, watching his preparations. Navarre looked up suddenly, hearing the clatter of hooves on cobblestones as someone rode toward them down the alley. He glanced at Imperius; he held his wrist up, signaling the hawk onto it. Imperius nodded, his face furrowing with worry, as Navarre handed the hawk carefully onto his own wrist. Navarre slipped out of sight behind the wagon.

The guardsman rode down the alley and into the cul-de-sac, unexpectedly finding it occupied by an old man in a cowled robe.

"Oh, thank goodness!" the old monk said, smiling at him in apparent relief. "Which way is it to the cathedral, my son?"

The guard's suspicious glance took in the monk standing with a hunting bird perched incongruously on his arm, the saddled, riderless war horse . . . the cart draped with a blanket.

He rode directly to the cart, ignoring the monk, and jerked the blanket aside.

Navarre lay waiting for him with a loaded crossbow. The guard reached for his sword, and Navarre fired. The guardsman toppled from his horse with the arrow through his heart.

Navarre leaped down from the cart, went to the body to pick up the guard's fallen sword. He hefted it, testing its balance; felt its edge with his thumb and swung it again experimentally. Imperius was wrong—just as he had known all along that the old man had to be. He had waited long enough; there was no use in denying fate any longer. He turned back, crossing to the stallion again with the sword in his hand.

Imperius blocked his path suddenly. "Navarre, don't be a fool! This chance will never come again!"

Navarre looked at him bleakly. "You're right, old man. The Mass will be over soon. If Phillipe has done his job, I can kill the Bishop now—or never." He raised his arm, and the hawk flew from Imperius's wrist to his own. He pushed past the monk to the stallion's side. Reaching into a saddlebag, he took out a small leather hood and jesses. He fitted the hood over the bird's head. The hawk cried out, suddenly blind, and dug her talons more deeply into his gauntlet for support.

Navarre turned back to the monk. "If the Mass ends peacefully and the cathedral bells begin to toll again—you will know I have failed."

"And . . . if I hear the warning bells?" Imperius asked.

"Either way—I'm a dead man."

"And . . . what then?" Imperius said carefully.

Navarre walked back to him, carrying the hawk; he handed him the jesses and Isabeau's dagger. "Take her life," he said. "Make it quick and painless."

Imperius drew back, appalled. "I can't do that," he whispered.

"Don't, then!" Navarre said furiously. "Let her live without me, and damn her to a half-life of eternal pain and misery!"

Imperius stared at him, stunned by the realization that the end had finally come, in spite of all his prayers, in spite of everything he had tried to do to stop it.

Navarre looked up at the clouds, and back at him again. "Have you ever considered, old man, that this was what God intended all along?" He handed the hawk to Imperius and turned away abruptly. Crossing to the stallion, he reached into a saddlebag again and pulled out his captain's helmet. He touched the golden wings briefly with his fingertips before he settled the helmet onto his head. Then he drew out Isabeau's blue silk dress, which he had carried with him for so long, a futile promise. Within its folds he found the lock of her hair that he had kept as well. He tore a strip of fragile cloth from the dress's hem; he tied the ribbon of cloth gently about the ringlet of her hair. And then he bound it to his left arm, next to his heart. He swung up into the saddle. Turning Goliath, he rode out of the alley without looking back.

Behind him, the hawk gave an anguished shriek as she sensed his departure. Navarre winced, feeling as if his heart were being torn out of him. He reached the alley end and turned into the street, heading for the cathedral.

Standing alone in the alley, Imperius bowed his head as Navarre disappeared. Remembering that this was the holy day of confession and repentance, he crossed himself and murmured, "Oh, Holy Father, deliver me from my sins, and these good people from the curse which afflicts them. You have seen fit to bring us all this far, and we humbly place our lives in the infinite mercy of Your everlasting grace."

Chapter Nineteen

The congregation of clergy stood in place at last in the great cathedral hall. A thousand small rustlings and shiftings filled the expectant silence as two acolytes slowly pushed the great doors shut. The Bishop's bodyguard fitted a heavy key into the gold-plated lock.

The recitation of the Mass began. As Phillipe heard the cathedral's hall fill with chanting voices, he pushed upward on the grating again. This time it did not budge. Startled, he sank back, peering up through the opening. A pair of knobby legs clad in bright red stockings, a cassock, and a walking stick were all that he could see. The Bishop's secretary was standing on top of the grate.

Phillipe pressed back against the sloping wall,

his fist tapping nervously on his drawn-up knees. How long had it been? How long could he stand to hang on here, waiting for this oaf to grow restless and move? He wiped his face with a grimy hand. What if Navarre was already on his way?

Silently he drew his dagger and pushed the blade up through the grate. Twisting it, he pricked the Bishop's secretary on the foot. One red-stockinged leg rose out of sight as the secretary scratched his ankle. The foot settled back onto the grating. Phillipe jabbed again, harder.

The secretary hopped aside with a yelp of pain and horror. Another pair of feet, sandals and a friar's white robe, rushed to his aid. "Sir! What is it?" the friar gasped.

"Rats!" the secretary said shrilly. He drove his walking stick down through the grate. Phillipe jerked back as it missed his face by a fraction of an inch.

"A scandal," the friar murmured. Phillipe listened to the sound of retreating footsteps with a sigh of profound relief. He looked up once more; his view of the rose window was completely clear. He pushed the grating aside and wriggled through into the unoccupied side chapel.

Crouching down, he looked toward the great doors at the rear of the cathedral, and frowned. It was too far away—he would never get that far unnoticed, looking and smelling the way he did. He glanced around the chapel nervously;

his eyes fell on a coarse white robe and a pile of baskets left in a corner by some hurried acolyte. He slipped quietly across the room and pulled the robe on over his muddy rags.

Picking up a basket, he drifted out into the gathering of clergy who stood patiently in the back of the crowded hall. Keeping his head bowed and holding the basket before him, he murmured softly, "Alms for the poor . . . God is watching . . . alms for the poor. . . ." Most of the clerics recoiled from him in mild disgust, but one priest flipped a coin into his empty basket.

Phillipe started in pleasant surprise. "Thank you, Father," he muttered. "Make a note of him, Lord. . . . Alms for the poor . . ." He moved on toward the door, biting the coin speculatively.

Outside in the square, Marquet looked up at the cloud-filled sky, trying without success to guess the hour, and whether it would rain. He sat with his troop before the cathedral, waiting. Navarre still had not come; and yet he was certain that his enemy was in the city. He felt it in his bones.

He glanced down as another of his guardsmen rode into the square to report on their search of the city. He returned the guard's salute impatiently.

"All the men have reported in, sir. Except Jouvet." The guard looked away uneasily. "We . . . can't find him."

Marquet frowned as his own unease increased

tenfold. He turned to his lieutenant, a youth he
had promoted into Jehan's position because he
knew how to obey orders—and because he had
never served under Navarre. "No one enters or
leaves this cathedral until the Mass is ended,
Lieutenant," he ordered. "You're in command
now." The lieutenant saluted eagerly. Marquet
turned his back on the young officer's enthusi-
asm and rode out of the square at a gallop.

Marquet cantered his stallion through the
streets, searching rooftops and doorways and
alleys as he rode toward the place where Jouvet
had last been seen.

And as Marquet rode away from the cathedral square, Navarre turned another corner; that
much closer to his meeting with destiny.

Inside the cathedral, Phillipe wove his way
through the last of the clergy at the back of the
hall. He slipped quietly behind a pillar, looking toward the heavy doors. Beside his knee on
the pillar's base a stone wolf stood on its hind
legs, peering eternally at something above his
head. Phillipe looked up curiously, and saw
the hawk carved on the pillar's capital, its wings
spread for flight, frozen in stone. Glancing away
down the hall, he realized that all the columns
in the vast cathedral were ringed with wolves
gazing up in eternal longing at flightless hawks.
Holy-day pennants of black-and-white silk
splashed with crimson hung suspended before

the pillars—the colors of the Church, the colors of life and death.

He shuddered, and looked back again at the heavy cathedral doors, his face set with determination. The carven faces of nameless saints watched him silently from niches along the walls. For the first time he actually saw the lock that he was here to open—gleaming gold, as massive and as solid-looking as the doors themselves. And just as exposed. He let his head fall back against the pillar, shutting his eyes for a long moment. Then, bending down, he pulled his dagger from his boot again with a sigh of resignation. Behind him, the entire congregation knelt down in a responsive prayer. Crouched low, he darted across the open space to the door. He stuck the dagger's tip into the keyhole and began to feel for the mechanism inside.

Meanwhile, Marquet rode slowly down another city street, nearing the place where Jouvet had last been seen. He glanced into one more of the endless alleyways as he passed; suddenly pulled his horse up short, frowning, and turned in. At its end he found the abandoned cart that had caught his eye, and the dead body of Jouvet. He dismounted and yanked the arrow from the dead man's chest. He studied the fletching and the bloody tip. Then he vaulted back into his saddle and galloped out of the alleyway, heading toward the cathedral, his gut feeling now a deadly certainty.

Behind him in the empty alley, Imperius peered out of a shadowed doorway with the hawk on his arm, his face lined with concern.

Phillipe worked desperately at the lock, getting nowhere. The mechanism was too large and stiff for the slim blade of his dagger to budge. But he couldn't fail now . . . he didn't dare. If he could only have a few more minutes, uninterrupted . . .

Behind him the congregation rose to its feet as the prayer ended. He straightened up and turned around, pressing back against the door. The clerics all still faced the altar, even the Bishop. He wiped his sweating face on his sleeve and turned back, probing the lock more mercilessly.

But one man in the congregation was not facing the altar. The Bishop's bodyguard stood discreetly to one side, his short sword hidden beneath his robes, his gaze scanning the crowd. His eyes widened with sudden interest at the unexpected sight of someone standing in the shadows by the doors. The figure was only dimly lit, but he could see enough to realize that whoever stood there had his back turned to the altar. The bodyguard put a hand on his sword hilt and began to drift slowly and unobtrusively through the edge of the murmuring crowd, heading for the rear of the cathedral.

Navarre rode out of the side street into the cathedral square. He reined in the stallion; he sat motionless, studying the familiar view of the cathedral's arched and curving walls of stone, the elite troop of mounted guardsmen fanned out across the square before him. He watched their faces freeze with disbelief as they spotted him; saw them glance at each other in sudden uncertainty. He knew most of the faces as well as they knew his. "*Navarre . . . Navarre. . . .*" He heard his name spread from man to man like a sigh.

Marquet was nowhere in sight, Navarre noted, with fleeting disappointment. The lieutenant in charge, a fresh-faced youth he did not recognize, looked right and left in open distress as he searched in vain for his captain.

Navarre started forward, Isabeau's token fluttering brightly against his black sleeve as he rode across the silent square. He halted the stallion again when less than twenty feet separated him from the line of guards.

The lieutenant swallowed visibly, his eyes riveted on Navarre's winged helmet. "Put away your sword, Navarre," he said, with creditable determination, meeting Navarre's gaze at last. "Then dismount. You are . . . my prisoner," he finished weakly, as Navarre stared at him, unmoving. The lieutenant glanced back over his shoulder, as if he were unsure even of how his men would respond to his orders.

Navarre searched the line of guardsmen with his own eyes, found them all staring at him, their faces tight with indecision. Navarre took a deep breath. "As your captain who was," he said, "and through God's Grace will be once again—as a man who treated each one of you with respect—I ask you to let me pass."

The line of men did not move; but he saw swords quietly lowered, and the tension ease in face after face. He started forward again.

"Stop where you are!" the young lieutenant shouted hoarsely.

Navarre did not stop.

The lieutenant's jaw muscles twitched. "I have my orders!"

Navarre kept riding. All at once the lieutenant raised his sword, spurring his horse forward. Navarre swung his own sword as the other man charged him and parried the lieutenant's clumsy blow easily. He jammed the hilt of his sword into the young officer's stomach, knocking him from the saddle; his free hand wrenched the sword from the lieutenant's grasp as he fell. The guardsman sprawled on the hard pavement, lay moaning with pain and surprise.

Navarre slung the captured sword out across the square toward the line of guards. He sat waiting, his head high, his eyes burning.

The line of guards parted silently, clearing his path to the cathedral doors. Looking straight ahead, Navarre urged Goliath forward toward the waiting entrance.

Behind the doors Phillipe worked frantically on the lock, as the muted sounds of challenge and battle reached him from out in the square. He heard the sound of iron-shod hooves ringing on the stone steps of the cathedral—heard the soft scrape of a sword being drawn behind him. He turned, and gasped as he saw the Bishop's hulking bodyguard almost on top of him, saw the bodyguard's sword rising above his head. He jammed his blade into the lock with a last desperate thrust.

The lock mechanism clicked open. Phillipe threw himself aside with a cry of triumph and terror as the bodyguard lunged forward.

The doors burst open, as Goliath reared and drove his forelegs against them. One of the swinging doors smashed into the bodyguard's head, knocking him senseless to the floor. Navarre rode into the cathedral.

Silence fell as the assembled multitude of clergy turned to gape at Navarre, aghast and uncomprehending. The Bishop turned slowly from the altar, staring at the rider in black who sat silhouetted at the entrance to his sanctuary. His pale eyes blinked and blinked again, refusing to accept the reality of the vision before him.

Navarre urged the stallion forward into the cathedral. Goliath's hooves rang hollowly in the excruciating silence of the hall as Navarre rode toward the Bishop.

Phillipe tore his eyes away from Navarre, looked out the entrance at the sky, searching for a sign of Imperius's promised change. The sky was covered with clouds, darker than any he had ever seen. Phillipe looked down again as he heard another rider approaching; he saw Marquet gallop into the square and pull up short, taking in all that had happened there at a glance. Digging in his spurs, Marquet came on toward the cathedral entrance, his eyes shining with bloodlust.

Phillipe pushed himself up and slipped out the entrance, bolting away across the square toward the warren of streets beyond.

Chapter Nineteen

Navarre swung the stallion around as he heard Marquet ride into the cathedral. Marquet pulled his mount up short just inside the entrance. The two men faced each other, their eyes deadly with hatred, each of them knowing that this would be the last time they ever faced one another. The two stallions pranced and pawed the smooth stones of the floor, feeling their riders' tension, waiting for the signal to charge.

Marquet's gray rose on his hind legs suddenly and lunged forward. Goliath reared up at Navarre's signal, as Navarre raised his sword and rode to meet his enemy.

Clergy scattered in panic-stricken disbelief as the two warriors turned the cathedral into a battleground. Navarre drove ferociously at Marquet as their horses met. Marquet parried his blow; sparks flew as steel met steel. Marquet's eyes were dark with rage as he hacked at Navarre's gold-winged helmet. Navarre's sword flew up to knock the blade aside; struck back before Marquet could recover his balance, slashing at his throat. Marquet flung up his arm; his brass-mailed overshirt turned the blow aside, but Navarre saw a thin line of fresh red stain its white sleeve. Fleetingly it occurred to him that the clergy gaping at them from every side must have no idea why they were fighting here. Let the clerics bear God's witness, and they would learn soon enough what injustice had driven him to commit murder in God's house. . . .

Phillipe ran back through the winding city streets, searching for the alleyway that Imperius had described to him, the place where he would find the monk's cart hidden. The sky was darkening even more as he ran, until it almost seemed to be twilight in the narrow, crowded lanes. Even the air was growing colder. He glanced up at the clouds again with anxious eyes; he had never seen a sky like this one.

Finally he reached the corner he had been searching for, and raced down the alley. He skidded to a stop as he saw the dead guard and the empty cart. There was no sign of Imperius or the hawk. It didn't matter—Navarre was the one who needed his help now. Phillipe dropped to his knees, groping up underneath the cart. His tense face broke into a grin as his hand found the hilt of Navarre's sword, wedged into the corner boards where he had hidden it two nights ago. He jerked it free and pulled it out. Holding the sword close, he ran back out of the alley toward the cathedral.

Inside the cathedral, Navarre lunged at Marquet, braced himself against the shock as Marquet parried his blow again. They both bled now from minor wounds, but neither one could land a crippling blow. Gasping with exertion, he grimly acknowledged to himself that they were far too evenly matched. He saw the gleam of fanaticism and fear behind the hatred in Marquet's eyes—and knew what drove Marquet almost as mercilessly in this battle as the need for revenge drove him. But Marquet was not his true enemy; Marquet was only an obstacle that he must get past now, to reach the Bishop. He must not lose his only chance.

He attacked Marquet again with all the murderous fury of his obsession. He drove past the other man's guard; his sword hilt struck Marquet's helmet, unbalancing him in the saddle. Goliath reared against the gray, horse and rider moving instinctively as one; Navarre slammed his blade down onto Marquet's. Marquet tumbled from the saddle, his helmet and sword flying away across the floor. Marquet's horse charged off down the hall.

Navarre swung Goliath around, lifting his sword for the stroke that would finish Marquet. But his eye caught an unexpected motion at the back of the cathedral. He glanced up, saw the Bishop's bodyguard stumbling toward the untended belfry to sound the warning.

Navarre turned Goliath back, forgetting Marquet as he saw the bodyguard reach for the ropes. Desperately he pulled his crossbow from his saddle and took aim, fired. The arrow stuck its mark, and the bodyguard fell with a scream. But as he fell, his thrashing body tangled in the ropes, and the bell began to toll.

Navarre froze in horror as he heard the warning bells, and knew what he had done—realized who else would hear those bells and carry out his final orders. "No, Imperius!" he shouted, as if his voice could drown out the sound of bells. "No!"

Imperius stiffened upright in the darkness of the doorway where he had taken refuge. The cathedral's bells tolled out across the city, sounding the alarm. Navarre had failed . . . they had both failed. The old monk sagged back against the wall, listening to the sound that he had prayed he would never hear. He looked down at the hooded hawk clinging blindly to his sleeve, at the dagger he held in his other hand; his eyes blurred.

"Lord God Almighty," he murmured, his voice

faltering, "I do not understand why this beautiful creature should have to pay for my sins with her life. I never meant harm to anyone, and yet I have caused so much. Your ear is deaf to me, but I beg you to listen to the final heartbeats of this good woman, and of the man she loved, and grant them their rightful places in the Kingdom of Heaven."

He raised the dagger to the hawk's breast with a trembling hand ... raised his eyes one last time, searching the leaden skies for a sign. Beyond the city roofs, high in the mass of gray, a tiny crack of blue appeared, as the clouds began to part.

Navarre sat motionless in his saddle for a moment that seemed eternal, stunned with grief. Marquet roused himself, scrambled up from the floor, searching for a weapon. He found his fallen helmet and caught it up, hurling it at Navarre.

Navarre came alive, dodging out of the helmet's path as it flew at his head. He looked around and up as something shattered high above him, saw a rainbow of colored glass shower down as the helmet smashed the rose window above the cathedral doors. Navarre gasped. In the jagged gap shone a patch of brilliant blue sky ... and the face of the sun, almost entirely covered by the disc of the moon. Awe filled him as he gazed up at the eclipsing sun; seeing at last the thing he had never be-

lieved he would live to see: a day without
night, a night without day. . . .

He heard the shouting and screams of the
terrified clergy, as more of them fled from the
cathedral out into the darkening square. The
bells continued to toll, announcing doomsday
. . . reminding him that this moment had come
at last, one moment too late.

Navarre turned back to the altar, where the
Bishop stood clutching his staff, alone and
unattended. The Bishop's mouth pulled back
in a rictus of a smile that might have been
fear, or cruel mockery. Navarre saw nothing
else; remembered nothing else but the need
to claim his vengeance. "Damn you!" Navarre
shouted furiously, both a curse and a promise.
"*Damn you to hell!*" He dug in his spurs, and
the black stallion bolted forward toward the
altar.

Seeing Navarre's intent, Marquet jerked the
pole of a black-and-white pennant free from its
socket. Running toward Navarre, he jammed
the tip of the pole into the floor and vaulted
through the air, smashing into Navarre's side.
Navarre fell from his horse, and both men
crashed heavily to the stones.

Navarre struggled to his feet, his helmet gone
now, along with his sword. He scrambled after
his weapon, as Marquet found his own sword
and caught it up. Marquet was staggering with
exhaustion; but so was he. Navarre pulled his

dagger, held it ready in his fist as he snatched up his sword and turned to face Marquet's attack. The clergy who had not fled into the square still huddled between the pillars of the arcades, praying for deliverance from the end of the world, or gaping at the two men like spectators at a bear-baiting.

Navarre drove at Marquet with every brutal trick he had ever learned in battle, using sword and knife and fists, desperate to make an end of the fight before the moment in which he must confront the Bishop passed and was lost forever.

Marquet fought back viciously, but he was fighting for his life now, and Navarre sensed his growing fear. Navarre's battering attack forced him back and back, until finally Navarre's sword hilt and fist smashed into Marquet's jaw, driving him to his knees.

Suddenly Marquet's stallion, spooked away from the entrance by the panic-stricken crowd, bolted back between them and knocked Navarre sprawling. Navarre's sword flew free as he fell, and shattered on the floor. Marquet looked toward the Bishop, a grin of cruel triumph spreading across his face.

"Kill him!" the Bishop shouted. "*Kill him!*"

Marquet started forward. Navarre struggled to rise, seeing his sword lying beyond his reach, broken in two. A sharp, piercing whistle drew Navarre's eyes away to the cathedral's darkened doorway. Phillipe stood there, holding a broadsword in his hand. He slung the weapon across the floor toward Navarre. With a kind of disbelief Navarre saw that it was his father's sword—the sword he had believed was lost forever, along with all hope. He scrambled toward it, but Marquet was there ahead of him, cutting him off. Marquet's foot lashed out, kicking Navarre in the face, knocking him backward. Marquet stood over his fallen enemy, his sword high. "You're dead, Navarre," he hissed. He brought the sword down.

Navarre rolled out from under the blow at the final second. The sword struck the floor, sending up chips of stone; Navarre rolled back, pinning the blade with his body, wrenching it from Marquet's grasp. His own hands closed over its hilt and jerked it free, swung it up with the same motion, and drove it into Marquet's chest. Marquet doubled over in agony, and collapsed on the floor beside him.

Navarre climbed slowly to his feet, breathing hard. "Who's dead now?" he muttered sourly, staring down at Marquet's motionless body. He had kept one promise to God. He glanced at Phillipe, standing wide-eyed in the doorway, and up at the rose window, where the sun's face had completely disappeared. He leaned down to pick up his father's sword; turned back, looking at the Bishop. Now he would keep his final vow.

The Bishop stood before the altar, staring in stupefied horror at the darkened face of the sun, and at him. Navarre strode down the length of the cathedral toward the altar, his sword in his hand.

Chapter Twenty

Navarre advanced on the Bishop, blind and deaf to the staring faces and stunned whispers on every side, possessed by the soul-deep need that consumed him now.

The Bishop stood like a statue of glittering ice in the candlelight. He held up his staff as Navarre halted before him, a sword's length away. "Kill me, Navarre," he warned, his voice brittle, "and the curse will go on forever."

Navarre's hand tightened over his sword hilt as his muscles tensed for a blow.

"Think of Isabeau!" the Bishop cried.

Navarre met his stare with empty eyes. "She's dead."

The Bishop's mouth fell open; for a moment Navarre saw the terrible void of his own loss

mirrored in the Bishop's eyes. His grief blazed
into sudden hatred, and he lifted his sword.

"Navarre!"

Navarre stopped, his arm frozen in midair,
caught inside a memory by the sound of a
voice he had thought he would never hear again.
He turned.

Isabeau stood in the cathedral entrance,
framed by blackness—alive, and radiant with
wonder at the miracle which had suddenly set
her free. She wore the lavender-blue silk gown
that she had worn the last time he had seen
her, before the curse had taken them; the gown
that he had carried with him and kept safe for
her these past two years. He touched the piece
of blue silk cloth bound around his arm, staring at her. Her eyes shone with love as she saw
his face. She gazed back at him, blinking like a
blind woman who had suddenly been given
sight.

Navarre watched her, transfixed, through the
endless moment as she began to walk toward
him. She moved slowly, as if she were still
uncertain of her own reality; but her smile grew
with every step she took that brought her closer
to him. Navarre drank in the sight of her, like a
man who had been lost in the desert and had
finally reached the sea.

Navarre turned back to the Bishop. His bloody
gauntlet caught the Bishop's wrist, staining the
perfect whiteness of his robe. Navarre's sword
point pressed hard against the Bishop's chest.

"Look at me," Navarre said, his voice deadly. "*Look at me!*"

The Bishop stared at him, his eyes white-ringed with fear.

"And now," Navarre whispered, "look at us." He caught the Bishop's jaw, swiveled his head until he faced Isabeau.

Isabeau stared back at them, still coming toward the altar. Midway down the length of the cathedral, a shaft of sunlight struck the floor in her path, as the sun began to emerge from behind the moon's face beyond the shattered rose window.

Isabeau hesitated, her eyes darkening with doubt. She moved forward again, resolutely, step by step. Navarre held his breath, felt the Bishop stiffen in his grip. At the far end of the cathedral Phillipe and Imperius watched Isabeau walk forward; the monk crossed himself silently.

The shaft of light grew wider as Isabeau stepped into it. Her body shimmered, absorbing the glow; caught in the moment when time stood still . . . and passing through it. She blinked again in astonishment, came on toward them, luminous with sunlight, her smile widening as she realized that she was truly and irrevocably human once more. Navarre gazed in awe at her, as he too realized that hope had at last become reality. He stepped down from the altar and ran to meet her; knelt before her as she came to him, and took her hands in his.

She clung to him, reaffirming her reality and

his own; and then she released his hands again
and moved past him toward the altar, toward
the Bishop. Her eyes burned with fierce triumph
as they met the pale, staring eyes of her tor-
mentor. She stood before him, holding his gaze
relentlessly, and opened her hand. In her palm
lay the jesses that held a hawk captive. She
dropped them at his feet, her face stiff with
contempt. She turned her back on him again,
and started away from the altar.

Behind her the Bishop's eyes darkened with
fanatical rage. He touched the base of his staff
with his foot, exposing the steel blade hidden
in its tip. Taking a step forward, he raised the
staff like a spear.

"Navarre!" Imperius shouted from the back
of the cathedral. "Look out!"

Navarre tore his eyes away from Isabeau, saw
the Bishop raise his staff behind her back.
Navarre flung up his own arm and hurled his
father's sword at the altar with all his strength.
It struck the Bishop through the heart, impal-
ing him against the altar, killing him instantly.
Isabeau turned back, staring in horror. She
looked at Navarre again; she ran to him, held
him close inside the circle of sunlight, with her
face buried against his chest.

A sudden murmur of awe and dread filled
the stunned silence all around them. Navarre
lifted his head, glancing back at the altar. He
stared in disbelief; Isabeau turned in his arms,
following his gaze.

The Bishop was gone. His robes hung in an empty cascade from the altar. Instead a scrawny, aging wolf stood before the congregation, peering around the hall with frightened, bewildered eyes. The wolf bared yellow fangs as it fled the altar and ran down the length of the cathedral, making a wide arc past the patch of light in which Isabeau and Navarre stood. It scuttled on through the ring of dumbstruck, gaping clergy with its tail between its legs, and disappeared past Phillipe through the waiting doors.

Navarre drew Isabeau to him again, holding her tightly. The circle of light widened around them, spreading outward like their own radiant joy. She laughed in delight as he swept her off her feet, dancing her around and around in the golden air. He set her down again, pulling her close once more, feeling her warm and real against his heart. He kissed her deeply, endlessly, their two bodies no longer as separate as night and day, but in that moment one, as their souls were one.

Phillipe threw his own arms around Imperius, hugging the old monk in ecstatic congratulation as he watched Isabeau and Navarre embrace at last. Imperius beamed with pride; Phillipe pulled his rumpled head down and kissed him, grinning. On every side Phillipe saw the gathered clergy smiling too, their own faces filled with relief and celebration as they watched the joyous couple embracing in the sunlight—knowing that they had witnessed the defeat of evil, the triumph of faith and love.

Isabeau and Navarre ended their kiss and broke apart, their hands still joining them together. Isabeau looked toward the cathedral entrance; her eyes found Phillipe's, and for one brief moment her radiant smile belonged entirely to him. Phillipe glowed as a sudden, shining pride filled him. Her own face filling with love and laughter, Isabeau winked at him.

Phillipe glanced down, blushing; looked up again with a wink of his own—to meet Navarre's eyes gazing coldly at him. His grin faltered, until he saw Navarre surrender to laughter. Phillipe's grin came back, wider than before. He watched Navarre and Isabeau hold each other close and kiss again inside the shower of golden light, and his smile widened until he thought it would never stop. He was happier in this moment than he had ever been in his life, and every moment of his life from now on would have to be measured against this one. He had lived the dream at last . . . and because of him, the dream had come true.

Epilog

Phillipe stood in the road beside Imperius's oxcart, watching Isabeau and Navarre ride away together. Their figures, on the ridgeline high above, were limned by the golden clouds of evening as they began their journey through the mountains toward Navarre's home. They would come back to Aquila in time, when Navarre returned to serve a new Bishop in his rightful place as Captain of the Guard. But for now they wanted only time to share alone together, in peace. They rode side by side at a lazy walk, their horses almost touching, their eyes only for each other.

They looked back together one last time, in farewell. Phillipe lifted his hand, smiling, while Imperius watched contentedly from his cart.

As Navarre and Isabeau looked ahead again, Phillipe's hand fell, and his smile faded; but the yearning lingered in his eyes.

Imperius looked down at him from the cart, shaking his head. "Don't worry, little thief," he said gently. "Your time will come." He glanced at the road ahead, and down at Phillipe again. "I'm heading back for the abbey." His smile widened. "To discover where the wind comes from. May I drop you somewhere along the way?"

Phillipe glanced on along the road at the sound of another cart approaching. He blinked, stared with sudden fascination. Coming toward them was a small wagon, driven by a young peasant girl with the face of an angel. Long honey-colored hair fell loose down her back, shining like gold in the light of the setting sun. "Actually," Phillipe murmured absently, "I'm headed in the other direction."

Imperius looked down at him with a firm but kindly gaze. "I fully expect to meet you at the Pearly Gates, little thief." He smiled again. "Don't disappoint me."

Phillipe grinned, and waved the monk a farewell as the oxcart lumbered off down the road. He turned back, glancing up at the ridge. The sun's fiery ball disappeared behind the line of the hill as he watched; he felt a sudden, familiar tightness fill his chest.

Up on the ridge, Navarre's expression darkened as he watched the sun sink behind the hills. Isabeau's hand clutched his arm in a painful grip, as the same unspoken thought filled both their minds. She was free of the curse . . . but was he?

Phillipe heard a wolf howl, somewhere in the hills. He shut his eyes, suddenly unable to keep watching; forced them open again, repeating a silent prayer. He looked up at the hills apprehensively. His eyes fell on a riderless horse; his heart missed a beat as he searched the ridgeline. Farther along it he found the black stallion—Isabeau and Navarre riding together, her arms wrapped around him, her face nestled against his chest. Phillipe whooped with triumph, his smile back to stay as he watched them ride on toward a new life.

Isabeau glanced back toward the valley with a grin as she heard Phillipe's shout. She looked up into Navarre's face again, filled with such happiness that she still could barely believe it was not a dream. Navarre kissed her hair tenderly, his eyes shining with contentment.

Goliath stumbled in the stony track. Isabeau steadied herself, putting her hand on the hilt of Navarre's sword. She glanced down as her fingers wrapped around it; saw the Bishop's emerald ring, which Phillipe had embedded in the empty socket at its top, the symbol of a quest fulfilled. Her hand adjusted comfortably around the familiar grip; her fingers shifted, searching, as they slipped into a sudden unfamiliar concavity. She looked down in curiosity, opening her hand. On the far side of the hilt was another empty socket. The emerald that Navarre's father had set into place had disappeared.

Navarre looked down at her sudden indrawn breath, and saw the empty socket. His eyes filled with realization, and then with outrage and dismay. He turned back in his saddle, glaring down into the shadowed valley.

"Damn you, Gaston! Damn you!"

Phillipe glanced up into the flaming colors of the sunset as he heard Navarre's shout mingling with the peals of Isabeau's delighted laughter. He looked down again, moving a little closer to the warm body beside his own on the wagon seat. He held the emerald out in the palm of his hand, watching the peasant girl's eyes, which were the color of sapphires, widen in awe. "It belonged to my mother," he said softly.

"It's . . . beautiful . . ." she whispered, gazing back at him in wonder, as he had always known she would.

"Actually," he sighed, "it's my only memory of her. . . ."

They rode on together, into the most beautiful sunset he had ever seen.

About the Author

JOAN D. VINGE was born in 1948 in Baltimore, Maryland. An avid science fiction reader since junior high school, she has been writing it professionally since 1973. She now lives in Chappaqua, New York, with her husband, Jim Frenkel, and their daughter, Jessica. Jim is the publisher of Bluejay Books.

Joan studied art in college, but eventually changed to a major in anthropology and received a B.A. degree in it from San Diego State University. She has worked as a salvage archeologist, and finds her background in anthropology has been very useful in writing science fiction. Anthropology is similar to science fiction in many ways—they both offer fresh viewpoints for looking at "human" behavior: archeology is the anthropology of the past, and science fiction is the anthropology of the future.

Her first story, "Tin Soldier," a novelette, appeared in ORBIT 14 in 1974, and her stories have also appeared in ANALOG, MILLENNIAL WOMEN, ISAAC ASIMOV'S SF MAGAZINE, and other magazines and anthologies, including several "Best of the Year" anthologies. Joan has six books out: PHOENIX IN THE ASHES, WORLD'S END, PSION, THE SNOW QUEEN, THE OUTCASTS OF HEAVEN BELT, and EYES OF AMBER AND OTHER STORIES. She has also written a children's storybook of THE RETURN OF THE JEDI, and a version of TARZAN for young adults, as well as the DUNE STORYBOOK.

Her story "Eyes of Amber" won the 1977 Hugo Award for Best Science Fiction Novelette, and her novel THE SNOW QUEEN won the 1981 Hugo Award for Best SF Novel. Joan has been nominated for several other Hugo and Nebula awards, as well as for the John W. Campbell New Writer Award. PSION was named a Best Book for Young Adults by the American Library Association. THE RETURN OF THE JEDI STORY-BOOK was the #1 Bestseller on The New York Times Book Review List for two months; it was the first such book to reach #1 on the list.

Great Science Fiction from SIGNET

Great Science Fiction from SIGNET

**Buy them at your local
bookstore or use coupon
on next page for ordering.**

More Science Fiction from SIGNET